# Jessie was crazy to have lunch with Adrian

Even if it was strictly business. But how could she keep her mind on business when every smoky gaze and every gesture would remind her of what they'd once shared?

She was twenty-eight now, not eighteen, she reminded herself. This was as good a way as any to prove to herself that it was over between them. And prove it she must, if they were now going to be neighbors.

Picking up her bag, she started for the door, then froze. She had forgotten one small detail—by living next door, Adrian would meet Sam. If he suspected that Sam was his son, he would go after him as single-mindedly as he'd assaulted Everest.

She had fifteen minutes to think of a way to stop him from making that discovery.

**Valerie Parv** had a busy and successful career as a journalist and advertising copywriter before she began writing for Harlequin in 1982. She is an enthusiastic member of several Australian writers' organizations. Her many interests include her husband, her cat and the Australian environment. Valerie's love of the land is a distinguishing feature in many of her books for Harlequin. She lives in New South Wales.

## Books by Valerie Parv

### HARLEQUIN ROMANCE
2896—MAN SHY
2909—SAPPHIRE NIGHTS
2934—SNOWY RIVER MAN
2969—CENTREFOLD
3005—CROCODILE CREEK
3125—LIGHTNING'S LADY

### HARLEQUIN PRESENTS
1229—MAN WITHOUT A PAST
1260—TASMANIAN DEVIL

# FAR FROM OVER
## Valerie Parv

## *Harlequin Books*

TORONTO • NEW YORK • LONDON
AMSTERDAM • PARIS • SYDNEY • HAMBURG
STOCKHOLM • ATHENS • TOKYO • MILAN
MADRID • WARSAW • BUDAPEST • AUCKLAND

Original hardcover edition published in 1991
by Mills & Boon Limited

ISBN 0-373-03209-9

Harlequin Romance first edition July 1992

FAR FROM OVER

# CHAPTER ONE

'ADRIAN? It can't be! Adrian?'

Jessie Cole didn't know she'd cried his name aloud until the taxi driver shot her a curious look over his shoulder. 'Are you all right, lady? You look as if you've seen a ghost.'

Maybe she had. She could have sworn that the man getting into the moss-green Jaguar ahead of them was her estranged husband, Dr Adrian Cole. But it couldn't be. Adrian had been dead for six years. She blinked rapidly as the green car accelerated away from them. 'I'm all right,' she assured the driver. She fumbled in her bag for his fare.

He accepted it, smiling his understanding. 'Jet lag does weird things to you. I remember after a trip to Disneyland with my kids I was as grouchy as a bear until my body caught up.'

She nodded absently, his words triggering fresh memories. Adrian had been a bear of a man, big and solid. Yet, for all his size, he had been whipcord-trim and moved with catlike grace. She always used to think of him in animal terms. Hair tawny-coloured as a lion's mane. A bear-like temperament and panther-quick movements. They all fitted the man she had seen getting into the car and driving away. She shook her head. The driver was right. Jet lag was getting to her.

The driver eyed her worriedly. 'I'll give you a hand with the luggage. You look as if you're out on your feet.'

'Thanks.' Proving his point, she swayed as she waited beside the taxi. When he'd stacked her cases on the footpath, she reached for them, but he insisted that she go ahead and open up.

He deposited her luggage inside the door and sniffed the herbal-scented air appreciatively. 'Smells better than my place did after two weeks away.'

'A friend kept it aired for me,' she explained.

'Makes all the difference.' He glanced around. 'Is there anything else I can do to help?'

'No, thanks. You've been very kind.'

He refused the money she tried to press into his hand. 'No need.' He took a deep breath. 'Maybe we could have dinner some time. Talk about our travels.'

It was said so tentatively that she wasn't offended. But she was confused. 'You said... your children...'

'You mean Disneyland? I was married then. Now they live with my ex-wife and I see them on weekends. It isn't the same somehow.'

Tiredness throbbed through her and she pressed a hand to her head. 'It's nice of you to ask me, but...'

'Another time, maybe when you aren't jet lagged.' He seemed to sense that there wouldn't be another time but didn't press the issue.

His gaze lingered on her trim figure which her dress-for-success linen suit couldn't quite disguise, travelled to her tangle of ash-brown hair, fluffed up from its classic pageboy into an airy, wind-blown look by an American hairdresser, and pursed his lips regretfully. 'Pity.' Then he closed the door behind himself and she was alone. Alone except for the haunting vision of a man getting into a car outside her house.

Adrian.

The driver's interest in her was eclipsed by the conflicting emotions which assailed her at the very thought of his name. But it wasn't Adrian. It couldn't be him ever again. Nevertheless, her heart pounded so hard that she felt ill, and heat flooded her limbs, making them tremble. The years hadn't made any difference to the way she responded at the mere thought of him. In her jet-lagged state, seeing his twin was almost more than she could handle.

Why did thoughts of him still affect her so powerfully? It wasn't as if she had lived a hermit's life since they separated. Men found her attractive enough, as the taxi driver had demonstrated. But she had to face facts. She dated for companionship. There wasn't a man alive who could fill the place Adrian had carved for himself in her life.

Jo nagged her about it constantly. 'You must stop comparing every man you meet to Adrain Cole. He's gone. And even if he weren't, I doubt whether he could live up to his own legend.'

Jo was right as usual. Jessie should stop making Adrian into something he wasn't, and probably never had been. As her friend pointed out, if he had been so wonderful they would still be married.

Stop this, her mind screamed. The strain of the last three weeks, working with a difficult Hollywood star whose tastes in decorating bordered on the bizarre, then checking out some business leads for herself, were taking their toll.

The long flight back to Adelaide, lengthened by a three-hour hold-up in Hawaii hadn't helped. Jessie felt punch-drunk. She eyed the pile of luggage with despair. Unpacking would have to wait. If she didn't lie down soon, she would fall down.

The phone shrilled and she groaned, tempted to let it ring. But it was probably Jo Drury—Napier now, she corrected herself mentally, reaching for the phone.

'Howdy, jet-setter,' came the cheerfully husky voice.

Hearing her best friend's Marlene Dietrich tones made Jessie feel better. 'Hello, Jo. I don't know about jet-setter. I'm just glad to be home. How's Sam?'

'Your son and heir is playing a video game with my daughter and heir. I'm surprised you can't hear them up in the Hills.'

'At least he isn't pining for me,' Jessie said, unable to suppress a twinge of resentment.

'He was, but I'm better at distracting than he is at pining.'

'No wonder you're such a good teacher. And a great house-sitter. The place looks wonderful.'

'No problem,' Jo assured her. 'There's food in the refrigerator and your bedroom's aired. I'll bring your mail when I return Sam tomorrow.'

Guilt assailed Jessie. 'Maybe I should come for him now.'

A tut-tut of disapproval clicked down the phone. 'He's fine right here. I told you before you left that it was time to loosen the apron-strings a little. Don't go regressing on me, now you're home.'

Jessie chuckled. 'You're right.' She yawned hugely. 'Would letting him say hello turn him into a mummy's boy?'

'Not if you keep it short. I'll get him.'

Propped against the wall, Jessie almost nodded off as she waited for Sam to come to the phone.

'Hi, Mum.'

At the sound of his voice she jerked upright. 'Hello, sweetheart. I just got back. How are you?'

'Good. I got all your postcards. The Hallowe'en one's the best. It glows in the dark.'

Which was why she had chosen it. 'I suppose by now you've worked out how it does that?'

'Of course.' His voice became serious as he explained the principles of fluorescence to her. It wasn't so startling unless you knew that Sam Cole was only six years old. She listened patiently for as long as she could keep herself awake, then asked him to put Jo back on the line.

'I should have asked before. How's married life?'

'Heavenly. Nell loves her new daddy, and so do I. There's a lesson for you here, my friend.'

The last thing Jessie needed right now was a lecture from Jo. She was glad her friend had found a man who loved her and her child equally, but it didn't mean it could happen to everyone. Jessie wasn't even sure she wanted it to. 'I'm glad it's working out,' she forestalled Jo. 'I have to go now or I'll fall asleep standing up.'

'I understand, but there's something you should know.'

Whatever it was, it would have to wait. 'We'll talk tomorrow.' Even to her own ears she sounded like a sleepwalker. 'Did I tell you I saw Adrian?'

'You what?'

'It wasn't him. But it looked just like him. He was getting into a car in the Grattons' driveway.'

'Go straight to bed this minute.' Jo sounded her schoolteacherish best. 'I'm taking the kids to see a new dinosaur film tomorrow, so we'll see you after lunch. You'll probably sleep till then anyway.'

'Probably. Kiss Sam g'night for me.'

'It's only four in the afternoon.'

'Not to me, it isn't.' Jessie fumbled the phone on to its cradle. Her eyelids drooped as she staggered to her room where she fell on to the bed, fully clothed. She was asleep almost before she landed.

Fragments of the past drifted through her dreams. She was a salesgirl again in the home decorating division of Grattons Department Store. Adrian, already well known as a television weatherman, had come into the store for advice on decorating his apartment.

The sight of him, so ruggedly masculine, yet so courteous, had made her heart race a mile a minute. It was an effort to keep her mind on the job. 'The decorator is at lunch. I can have her paged in the staff canteen.'

'In matters of taste, I'm sure your advice is as valid as hers,' he assured her.

She found herself wanting to help him. Quizzing him about his lifestyle gave her the chance to get to know him a little, in the line of duty, of course.

Shyly, she gave him some suggestions based on the information he supplied. He must have liked her ideas because he returned a day later and ordered a small fortune in soft furnishings. His first dinner invitation coincided with her promotion to assistant decorator.

Several more dates followed, until her nights were filled with dreams of him. Her heart was just starting to rule her head when he announced that he wouldn't see her for several weeks. 'I'm attempting to climb the south-west face of Everest,' he told her, his eyes glowing with enthusiasm.

Icy fingers gripped her heart and squeezed it until she felt faint. The thought of him clawing his way up a notoriously inhospitable mountain terrified her. 'Isn't it dangerous?'

'Of course. It's partly why I do it.'

Jessie tossed restlessly in her sleep, wanting to wake up but held in thrall by her dreams. She hadn't woken up then, either, waiting dutifully while Adrian made his assault on Everest, before coming home to take up where they left off.

Then came an expedition to Mawson's Hut in Antarctica to report on cloud patterns for science, followed by caving in New Britain to establish whether the islands of Papua New Guinea were the cradle of Pacific civilisation.

When he returned from this last expedition, sheer relief prompted her to accept his proposal of marriage. For a while he seemed content to be a married man, pursuing his career as a television meteorologist. The days were filled with interest and the nights with magic. He was a considerate but passionate lover who made every night a honeymoon.

Then he decided to be the first man to canoe the entire length of the Jardine River in rugged far north Queensland.

'I'll be dropped into the headwaters by helicopter,' he told her with a now-familiar gleam in his eyes.

Terror gripped her. She was married to a madman. Her pleas moved him not an inch. She was sure he didn't believe her when she threatened to be gone by the time he returned.

Leaving was the hardest thing she had ever done. Two years of marriage had convinced her that there was no other man in the world for her but Adrian Cole. Which was why she couldn't bear another minute of waiting to hear that he'd killed himself.

'You knew what I was when you married me,' he railed when he traced her to a friend's apartment.

'I thought you'd stop this craziness once we were married.'

'So it's craziness, is it? I suppose I should have a nine-to-five job with retirement benefits.'

'At least you'd live long enough to retire.'

His mouth tightened into an implacable line. 'Some life it would be, shackled to your apron strings.'

Stricken, she stared back. 'No, I didn't mean ...'

'Didn't you? Face it, Jessica, you want a lap-dog who'll obey your every command. And that's what you get if you try to rein me in.'

Bitterness welled inside her. How could she make him understand that her concern was for him? She loved him too much to let him go on these insane quests.

But they were like two aliens speaking different languages. 'No one's going to rein you in,' she said tiredly. 'Not me nor a team of wild horses. You'll do what you want to do, as you always have.' She could see now that marrying her had been another challenge. Having conquered her, he needed new obstacles to overcome.

'If I could do what I want, I'd throw you into my car and take you home with me right now.'

Only because she was resisting him, she realised. 'It won't work, Adrian. It's over, finished.'

His eyes flashed fire. 'Is it? I can't believe you'd sacrifice what we have...had,' he corrected himself, 'because you can't have your own way.'

She could no longer hold back the tears. It was an effort to speak through the choking sobs. 'Is it so selfish to want your husband safe and well at home?'

'Not if the price is his manhood.' He started towards the door, turning when he reached it. 'I never planned on marriage, Jessica, but you were special. You seemed to understand my need for new frontiers. You had dreams of your own when we met. What happened to them?'

She didn't answer and she knew he was remembering her ambition to head Grattons' decorating division one day. But she had resigned altogether soon after they were married, telling herself he needed her at home.

'Living is risky,' he went on, his voice icy. 'I thought you'd scale the heights with me, not try to drag me down.'

'I love you,' she protested in a small voice.

'If you did, you would understand.' He wrenched the door open and stood framed in it, speaking almost as if to himself. 'I hope one day you want something for yourself, Jessica, and someone takes it away from you. If there's any justice in this life, that someone will be me. Then you'll know how much it hurts.'

His curse stayed in her mind for months after he left, its implications all the more chilling when she discovered that she was pregnant with his child. Would he make good his vow and take the child away from her? But he'd been in New Guinea during most of her pregnancy, and had left for Central Africa straight afterwards.

By the time Sam was born, Adrian had been missing for several months. With no word from him in the six years since then, he was believed to have died in the jungle. He never knew he had a son.

A vision of Sam, so childish in body yet so advanced in mind, filled her thoughts and a smile spread across her face. What would she have done without Sam during the agonising wait for news of Adrian? Although they were separated, she searched the papers for news of him, her pulses racing every time he was mentioned. She had cried for days after reading that he was dead. Only Sam's need of her had kept her going.

Progressing in leaps and bounds, he had kept her busy finding new challenges for his fertile brain, leaving her little time to wallow in unhappiness.

Even without a genius for a son, her friend Jo would have kept her spirits up. Sharing the same ward, they'd had their babies within hours of each

other, growing closer when they found they were
both alone. 'Thorne was in the police rescue
service,' Jo informed Jessie matter-of-factly. 'He
was trying to free the driver of a semi-trailer when
the rig rolled back on to him.'

'Oh, Jo, how terrible for you.' Jessie's knuckles
whitened as she gripped the edges of the bed.

'I lived with the possibility for years. But it
doesn't make it any easier when it happens. I just
thank the Lord I have Nell to remember him by.'

There but for the grace of God, Jessie thought.
Except that Jo's husband hadn't squandered his life
in a pointless search for adventure. He died trying
to save a life. She thought of Adrian in Africa. How
could he possibly justify the risks he took?

By the time she knew that he was presumed dead,
she had moved into Jo's semi-detached cottage in
Adelaide. They shared expenses and baby-sitting
and buoyed one another up when the going got
rough. She didn't know how she would have survived losing Adrian if it hadn't been for Jo. Now
her friend had remarried, this time to a fireman
who'd worked with her late husband. Some people
never learned.

But she had. Never again would she entrust her
heart to any man. 'Never, never,' she moaned,
thrashing from side to side.

Her eyes flew open and she lay still, waiting for
the thumping of her heart to subside. Where was
she? Then she remembered. She was in her own
bed and it was mid-morning. Her bedside clock
showed that she had slept for a full nineteen hours.

She'd been dreaming about Adrian, she realised.
Seeing his double must have opened the floodgates

of memory. A couple of times, she could have sworn she had heard his voice in her sleep.

A man's voice floated up to her through the partially opened bedroom window and she stiffened. It *did* sound like him. Maybe she only thought she was awake when really she was still dreaming.

This had to stop, she decided, swinging her legs over the side of the bed. A hot shower would make her feel human again. Stretching, she ambled to the window and pulled up the shade.

'Good grief!' The exclamation was ripped from her throat as she looked at the garden. Her small two-storey cottage was the former gatehouse of a larger estate, Gratton Park. It stood on a matchbox-sized block of land in a corner of the estate, separated from the larger parcel by a row of azalea bushes.

Or at least it had been when she left three weeks ago. Now it was cut off from the estate by the ugly bulk of a six-foot-high brick wall, the tiny size of her garden painfully apparent now that it was walled in on two sides. A third wall would soon cut her off from the estate completely, judging from the building activity going on below. It must have been the voices of the builders she had heard in her dreams. What on earth was going on?

'I'm hired to build a wall, I build a wall,' a man in checked shirt and overalls told her when she repeated the question to him a little later. She had stopped only long enough to pull on jeans and a sweatshirt, before racing downstairs to confront these vandals.

'There must be some mistake. I can't believe the Grattons would do this to me.'

Her former boss, Sir Mark Gratton, and his wife, Susan, were her friends. She had bought the gatehouse from them a year ago, after Jo had announced that she was marrying Chris and selling her house. Jessie had known the Grattons much longer, of course, having worked at their department store when she met Adrian.

Sir Mark was an old-fashioned man who treated his employees as family. When he'd found out that she had none, he had offered to give her away himself. With no children of their own, the Grattons had all but adopted Jessie and Adrian. They were as saddened as real parents would have been by the separation, but refused to take sides, offering their friendship to both impartially. It was hard to believe the wall could be their doing.

Getting nowhere with the builder, she decided to go and see the Grattons herself. Her path through the garden was walled off, forcing her to take the long way round by the road and along the driveway to the main house.

The place was in uproar. Scaffolding climbed over the Georgian exterior and black and yellow striped temporary power cables swung from the eaves. Power tools buzzed like frenzied insects, operated by soldier ants of workmen who ignored her when she marched past.

When had Susan Gratton decided to renovate? She'd talked about it but had never been able to spare the time from her charity activities. Something must have happened while Jessie was away.

The doorbell had been disconnected but the double cedar doors stood open. Jessie took a tentative step inside. 'Susan? Mark?'

There was no answer. Through the library door on her left, she heard voices and looked in. 'Excuse me.'

Two men were poring over plans which lay half unfurled on the great oak table around which she and Susan had spent many hours discussing books. One of the men looked up as she came in. 'About time.' He nudged the other man. 'Someone about the tiles at last.'

'I'm not from...' Her voice trembled into silence as the second man turned. This time there was no mistake.

He looked equally shocked. 'Jessica?'

'It *is* you, isn't it? I'm not dreaming.'

'Not unless we both are. What on earth are you doing here?'

'I live here. But you ... you're dead.'

He raised an eyebrow. 'I assure you, I'm not going to all this trouble just to haunt the place.'

She eased her death grip on the doorframe. 'It's no joking matter. All these years, I've believed you were dead. I feel as if I'm seeing a ghost.'

He took in her white face and trembling limbs. 'You're serious, aren't you? You haven't seen any of the newspaper stories?'

'I've been out of the country for three weeks.' She pressed her hands to her face and slumped against the wall. It *had* been Adrian getting into that car. Somehow, some way, he had survived and fate had brought them together. She felt weepy and elated all at once. And not nearly ready.

He moved to her side. 'Are you all right? I'll get you some water.'

Her hands slid down her cheeks and she met his eyes. They were the same smoky hazel she remembered, but a new network of lines radiated from the corners. Under his deep tan she detected dark smudges under his eyes. 'I can't believe it,' she said on a sighing breath.

'It's a long story and I'm sure you don't want to hear it now,' he said with an edge of cynicism in his voice. 'But I am sorry for scaring you. I thought my return was common knowledge by now.'

'It probably is, to everyone but me.' Her composure was returning. She sipped the water he fetched for her and a shudder rippled through her. 'What I don't understand is what you're doing *here*. Are Mark and Susan away?'

His eyes narrowed. 'You don't know, do you? They sold the place to me and moved into a retirement villa in Adelaide.'

'How could they do all that in three weeks?'

'They can do it in three days if the lawyers cooperate.' He raked long fingers through his hair which was even more tawny-gold than she remembered. 'God, don't tell me *you're* the owner of the gatehouse?'

Her answering nod was accompanied by a bleak look. 'Susan didn't tell you? No, of course she didn't. She knew you wouldn't buy the place with me living next door.'

'Still the matchmaker, isn't she? The Grattons were the first people I contacted after I got back. She never even mentioned you. I thought it was odd at the time.'

'And now you know why.'

'Yes. Susan obviously didn't know she was playing with fire.'

'I didn't see a need to tell them any more about the break-up than I had to.'

'Charitable of you. But then it wouldn't have shown you in a good light, either, would it?'

A feeling of despair gripped her. Five minutes in each other's company and already they were sniping at each other. 'I don't need this,' she said stiffly. She gestured apologetically to the other man who watched them awkwardly, fiddling with a corner of his plans. 'I'm sorry for intruding.'

'Did you want to see Mark and Susan? I'll give you their new address.'

Belatedly, she remembered why she was here. 'Thank you. But it isn't what I came for. It's about the wall you're putting around my garden.'

'I thought I was putting one around mine,' he said mildly.

'The effect is the same. You have to stop.'

His eyebrow arched ironically. 'Because you say so?'

'Because it's the right thing to do. Or isn't the word in your vocabulary?'

'Nothing changes,' he said as if talking to himself. 'Doing the right thing invariably means doing it your way, doesn't it, Jessica?'

She lifted open palms to him in a gesture of supplication. 'Adrian, please. Until five minutes ago, I thought you were dead. Let's not reopen old wounds.'

Lines of tiredness were etched into his face suddenly, as if the encounter had drained him, too. 'You're right. It's a poor way to say hello. Why don't we go and have some lunch and discuss the problem in a civilised way?'

At the thought of being alone with him, panic gripped her. 'I'm not dressed to go out.'

His sweeping glance encompassed the jeans hugging her narrow hips and the sweater which made it obvious that she wore no bra underneath it. 'You look fine to me, but then you always were a beautiful girl.' His smoky gaze softened fleetingly. 'Now you're a beautiful woman.'

Self-consciously, she brushed the fringe away from her eyes. 'You've been in the jungle too long.'

'Maybe. But you *are* beautiful. You're thinner and it suits you. And you've done something to your eyes.'

'I had the lashes dyed.' Her eyebrows had always been too pale to do much for her blue eyes which were rimmed with grey around the irises. The extra colour made them seem larger and more luminous. She was foolishly pleased that he had noticed, then she chided herself for her vanity. His opinion had ceased to matter a long time ago, or so she had thought. It was unnerving to find he could still bring a flush of pleasure to her cheeks.

'Well, what about lunch?'

She gestured towards the other man. 'I'm interrupting.'

'David has a lunch date of his own, haven't you?'

The other man grinned. 'Architect to architect. Strictly business.'

'Except that she's blonde and gorgeous,' Adrian said knowingly. 'We can finish this tomorrow.'

'In that case, I'll go home to change and meet you in front of the house in fifteen minutes.'

David, the architect, shot Adrian an envious glance. 'Lucy would need at least forty-five minutes.'

'So would Jessica, once.'

She fled, telling herself that she was crazy to have lunch with Adrian, even if it was—in the architect's terms—strictly business. How could she keep her mind on business when every smoky gaze and every gesture would remind her of what they had once shared? It was hard enough accepting that he was alive, without putting her hand into the flame of their former relationship.

She was twenty-eight, not eighteen, she reminded herself. With care, she wouldn't get burned, she told herself as she dressed. This was as good a way as any to prove to herself that it was over between them. And prove it she must if they were going to be neighbours.

Picking up her bag, she started for the door, then froze. She had forgotten one small detail. Living next door, Adrian would meet Sam. If he suspected that Sam was his son, he would go after him as single-mindedly as he assaulted Everest. She had fifteen minutes to think of a way to stop him from finding out.

## CHAPTER TWO

THE Jaguar was parked outside, and Adrian moved swiftly to open the door for her. Not knowing where they were going, she had chosen a georgette suit with wing-collared blouson and slim cropped skirt. As she got into the car, she was uncomfortably aware of the vast amount of tanned leg the skirt revealed.

Adrian made no comment. She wasn't sure he even noticed. He seemed preoccupied as he settled into the driver's seat and snapped his seatbelt taut.

'Nice car,' she said conversationally.

He gave a dismissive shrug. 'It was the quickest lease deal I could put together.' The engine purred and he glanced at her. 'I'm out of touch. Where would you like to have lunch?'

'The Beaker Full, off the Norton Summit Road, is supposed to be good. It's new since you . . .' She nearly said died.

He sensed her near slip. 'I haven't been resurrected—you can say it,' he said, with brittle humour.

She clenched her hands together. 'I'm still getting used to the fact that you're alive, far less here beside me. I can't help thinking it's part of my jet lag and I'll wake up and find I'm dreaming.'

'You can't wake up to find you're dreaming,' he said with maddening logic. 'But I assure you I'm real. Touch me.'

Rather than risk his scorn by refusing, she ran her hand along his forearm to where his long fingers rested easily on the steering wheel. He was wearing an olive army-style shirt with the sleeves rolled back and she felt a *frisson* of shock as his male hair brushed her fingertips. Her wide-eyed gaze went to his face, then back to the dark hairs curling possessively over his watch-strap. For a fleeting moment, envy for the watch consumed her. How would it feel to nestle in that warm, soft place?

She dragged her thoughts away and focused on the firmness of muscle and bone under his shirt. There was a new toughness about him, honed in the jungle. His flesh barely yielded to the pressure of her fingers.

'Now do you believe I'm real?'

She averted her gaze. 'I never really doubted it.' So why the compelling urge to touch him? Again, she had that moth-to-the-flame sense of living dangerously. They could have said all they needed to say to each other at Gratton Park. She should never have agreed to come out with him.

Her surroundings finally impinged on her consciousness. 'Where are we? This isn't the Norton Summit Road.'

He pulled up, and his fingers beat an impatient tattoo on the steering-wheel. 'Damn! I thought I took a wrong turning a mile back. To think I can find a *boma* in the middle of the African veld, yet get lost looking for a restaurant in the Adelaide Hills.'

She shot him a curious glance. Maybe he wasn't as impervious to her as he pretended. He was probably regretting the invitation as much as she was. 'Let's go back,' she urged. 'I'm not all that hungry.'

'No need.' He gestured along a side road. 'Isn't that the Beaker Full?'

Her heart sank as she recognised the restored nineteenth-century stables shaded by giant Moreton Bay fig trees. 'Yes, that's the place.'

He parked in the shade of a tree. Inside, it was cool and dim, the thick bluestone walls enclosing them intimately, the effect enhanced by a massive open fireplace, wide wooden roof beams and gingham tablecloths. It was the ideal place for an intimate lunch for two. She must have been mad to suggest it.

Adrian strode to the fireplace—unlit at this time of year—and read out the embroidered motif framed above the mantelpiece. '"O! for a beaker full of the warm South." John Keats. So that's where they get the name.'

As the only customers, they were shown to a window-table, which looked out across a smoky green expanse of bushland where jewel-coloured lorrikeets searched the dusty ground for food.

He regarded the vista with appreciation. 'It's good to have the bush around me again. The city takes some getting used to when you've been away.'

'After Africa?'

He nodded.

'Where *have* you been all this time?'

It wasn't meant as a criticism but a testy note entered her voice, and his mouth tightened in response. 'I didn't mean to criticise,' she hastened to add. 'I would like to know.'

'Why should you care? No, strike that, it's a fair question. I went to Central Africa with the idea of recreating Livingstone's travels along the Zambezi to the Kambompo confluence. Not too wisely I was alone, and rolled the Land Rover in a *donga*—a bloody great ditch,' he explained in answer to her questioning look. 'There was no serious damage—except to the vehicle—and I was taken in by some Luvale people. I had concussion and they took care of me. When I recovered, I decided to stay a while to repay the favour.'

'Six years is more than a while.'

He shrugged. 'There was a lot to be done. I taught the adults English, helped the children with their schoolwork, and showed them some good old Aussie farming tricks. Their land is a lot like ours—a sandpit for half the year and a swamp for the other half.'

The thought of him living a peaceful village existence while she waited for news of him made her anger rise. 'Couldn't you let someone know you were all right? Was it fair to let everyone think you were dead?'

The ferocity of her attack was answered by the sparks of annoyance which lit his gaze. 'The only "everyone" was you and you'd already made your feelings clear. The property split was in hand. If you were worried about the bit of paper...'

She saw what he was thinking. 'It wasn't a divorce I wanted, if that's what you mean. We were married for two years, for heaven's sake! You don't stop caring about someone so easily.'

His eyebrow arched. 'You managed to.'

Her lashes dropped as she lowered her head. 'I explained my reasons to you.'

'Oh, yes, I wasn't being a good little lap-dog, staying at my mistress's heel.'

Her sigh rippled between them. So much for civilised discussion! She was thankful when a waitress spread menus in front of them. Reading them allowed some of the tension to dissipate. 'The Coffin Bay rock oysters are good,' she said, 'and I'll have the whiting caprice.'

'The oysters and the crab mayonnaise,' he said, handing the menu to the waitress. 'Wine?'

She was having enough trouble controlling her errant emotions without wine making it more difficult. She shook her head. 'Not for me, thank you.'

He ordered Perrier for them both, then sat back, his eyes roving over the bushland outside the window. When he drew his gaze back to her, she was ready for him. 'Why did you come back?'

The silence stretched between them. 'I met some TV people making a documentary out there. They persuaded me to give civilisation another try. Besides, I had some unfinished business.'

Before she could ask him what he meant by this last remark, he leaned forward. 'I've told you what I've been doing for the last six years. How about you?'

Thinking of Sam, she looked away. 'Nothing much.'

'You said you were overseas when I got back. Where? Doing what?'

A spark of pride flared within her. The more he knew about what she'd been doing, the more chance there was that he would stumble on the truth about

Sam. But she was proud of what she'd achieved since they'd parted. 'I went back to Grattons,' she said softly.

'In sales?'

'As assistant head of department, then as chief decorating consultant,' she informed him, unwillingly thrilled by the light of respect which dawned in his eyes. Let him accuse her of lacking ambition now.

She didn't mention that it had been two years after their separation before she had summoned the courage to ask Grattons for her old job back. After Sam was born, postnatal depression had gripped her. It had taken all of Jo's cajoling to convince her that an employer would want her. As it turned out, Jo had been right. 'Of course it isn't Grattons any more, except in name,' she explained, since he probably didn't know.

Adrian surprised her by nodding. 'Sir Mark told me he retired two years ago. He didn't even want a seat on the board once the store passed out of family hands.'

'He was right. After the take-over, it wasn't the same. It became totally profit-driven and less of a people place.'

His curious gaze bored into her. 'Yet you stayed.'

'Not because of the money. I had a contract. And I'd built up something of a reputation as a decorator to the stars.' She had to give Adrian credit for that, she supposed: he was her first 'celebrity' customer.

When she said so, he shook his head. 'Your achievements are your own.'

'It's nice of you to say so. I was afraid you'd think I was trading on your name.'

'I'm surprised you still use it.'

'I'm not ashamed of being married to you, Adrian,' she said with such intensity that she surprised herself. She had always thought she kept her married name for Sam's sake. Could she have had a subconscious agenda of her own?

The arrival of their food was a welcome diversion. They occupied themselves with small talk and the business of eating.

She was achingly aware of every move he made, from the way he squeezed lemon juice over his oysters to the almost aggressive spearing of each succulent piece of shellfish, as if he were back in the jungle, hunting for his food.

'My trip was to California,' she said, to divert her thoughts. She named an American pop star who had seen her work during an Australian concert tour. 'He paid all my expenses to go over and pick out the furnishings for his place in Malibu,' she finished. Surely he would be impressed now?

'Quite the high-flyer these days, aren't you?' was the only dry comment he made before changing the subject. 'When did you buy the gatehouse?'

'A year ago,' she said tensely, aware that this was dangerous ground. 'Susan and Mark were keeping it for a goddaughter who changed her mind about living there and settled on the coast. I was stunned when they offered me the house at a price I could afford.'

Adrian toyed with his food. 'They were probably lonely after the hustle and bustle of running the store. You did them as much of a favour as they did you.'

'I hadn't thought of that. I was just grateful to be living in my own place.'

His sober expression echoed hers. 'It was a wise move. I gather you were renting until then.'

Jessie sensed danger ahead. Say too little and she would arouse his suspicions. Say too much and she jeopardised her future with Sam. 'It wasn't all bad,' she dissembled. 'Jo's house was small but comfortable.'

It was as if she'd given him the opening he'd been waiting for. His lip curled into an all-knowing sneer. 'Joe was your lover, I take it?'

She felt her colour heighten as she realised that he thought Jo was a man. It was on the tip of her tongue to disabuse him when some instinct warned her not to. Maybe she had been shown a way out of her dilemma after all. 'It *has* been six years,' she said lightly.

'From the sound of things, you haven't exactly wasted them,' he said grimly. Jessie could feel his anger reaching out to her across the table, like the radiant heat from a banked fire. She flinched from the intensity of it, but it was too late to retract now. Even if she told him Jo was a woman—and married at that—he was unlikely to believe her.

'I thought we were going to talk about the wall,' she said tensely.

He waited until their table was cleared and coffee was brought before answering her. 'There really isn't much to talk about.'

'You can see the size of the land around the gate-house. If it weren't for the view across Gratton

Park, it would be like living in a concrete prison,' Jessie objected.

'You should have considered that when you bought it.'

Despair welled up inside her. 'The problem didn't exist when I bought it. How was I to know the Grattons would sell up and move away without warning? I still don't know why they did it.'

He helped himself to cream and sugar with a generosity which suggested he had been denied them for a long time. 'No doubt Susan thought she was doing us a favour,' he said, stirring a white whirlpool into the black brew.

The swirling liquid held her gaze until she tore her eyes away. 'All the same, she could have warned me that they planned to sell up.'

'Maybe they wouldn't have moved out if I hadn't mentioned wanting to buy a place where I could work in peace. Knowing those two, Mark would have resisted, saying you should be told. Susan would have convinced him it was a fairy-tale situation.'

Except that there was no happy ever after. Jessie didn't blame Susan for doing what she thought was right. It was probably her own fault for letting them think the separation had been more amicable than it was. 'All the same, I can't let you build that damned wall,' she insisted.

His hard gaze glittered and his mouth twisted into a mocking smile. 'You still don't get it, do you? You can't control what I do but you don't know when to quit trying.'

'It isn't a power struggle,' she protested. 'It's not some kind of battle of wills. Our whole lifestyle is at stake.'

Instant interest flared in his expression. '*Our* lifestyle?' Then he clapped his palm to his forehead. 'Susan mentioned that the owner of the gatehouse had a child, which was why I didn't suspect anything. You and Joe didn't waste any time, did you?'

'There's no need to be crude about it,' she said, stung by the derision in his voice.

'Why not? When we were married, you refused point blank to give me a child. Yet you didn't waste any time throwing your blasted pills away as soon as you were free of me.'

'It wasn't like that. I was terrified of being left a widow, bringing up a child on my own because you'd thrown yourself off some God-forsaken mountain top.'

Ironically, she had stopped taking precautions when she'd thought he had finally settled down. Then he had broken the news that he was planning yet another dangerous adventure. By then it was too late. By the time she knew she was pregnant, they were separated and he was off in the wilds of New Guinea.

'Does Joe live with you in the gatehouse?' Adrian asked, in a dangerously low monotone.

'No. There's just me and Sam, my little boy.'

'Was it a fling, a rebound thing?' he asked.

Would it make any difference if it had been? 'No, it wasn't a fling,' Jessie said. 'I loved Sam's father.' This, at least, was the truth.

Something seemed to die inside Adrian. His eyes darkened, as if a flame had gone out behind them.

'I didn't mean to cross-examine you,' he said. 'It must be rough, bringing up a kid on your own.'

'It's hard at times,' she admitted cautiously, not sure how to react to the sudden cessation of hostilities. 'But it has its compensations. Sam is a joy— a joy with an IQ of a hundred and thirty,' she added wryly.

He whistled softly. 'Smart kid. Keeping up with him must be a challenge.'

No harder than keeping up with his father had been, she mused. Dr Adrian Cole could be accused of a lot of things, but stupidity wasn't among them. Intellectually, he was one of the smartest people she knew. It was easy to see where Sam got his brains from. But in looks he was all hers, a fact for which she was thankful now. At least Adrian wouldn't discern his parentage by looking at Sam.

'You've changed,' he observed thoughtfully. 'You're more sure of yourself than I remember.'

'More grown-up, don't you mean? Motherhood doesn't give you much choice,' she said acidly.

Adrian looked pensive. 'Maybe Sam's father found the key. God knows I tried and failed.'

She toyed with her coffee, finding it too strong to drink after all. 'Nobody failed, not you, not me. Maybe getting married was the mistake. If so, I'm as much to blame as you are.'

His eyes met and held hers across the table and she saw his fingers tighten as if he was keeping his temper in check with an effort. 'However it turned out, I don't regret marrying you, Jessica. What we had was pretty special, even if you refuse to admit it.'

Her eyes slid away from his. If she admitted it, she would also have to admit that he was still the only man in her life. Jo was right. She still compared every man she met to Adrian Cole, and there was simply no comparison.

But that didn't mean she could go on living with him, torturing herself with thoughts of him off on some crazy adventure. How could any woman live with that? How did astronauts' wives cope?

When her gaze returned unwillingly to him, her expression was bleak. 'We had this discussion six years ago. It didn't get us anywhere then.'

'And nothing's changed.' He glanced at his watch. 'I have to get back. I'm expecting a business call.'

He had shut her out and it was no more than she deserved after making it clear that she had nothing to say to him. Yet she was loath to let him go. 'You mentioned buying Gratton Park so you'd have somewhere quiet to work. What are you working on?'

He gave a mocking half smile. 'You'd approve of this project. I'm writing a book about my experiences in Central Africa. And I'm putting together some material for an armchair adventure series for the producer who lured me back here.'

'Sam will love that. He——' She clamped her mouth shut on the betraying words she had nearly said—he takes after you. 'He loves travel documentaries,' she substituted.

'A trait worth encouraging,' he agreed, but she could see that he had lost interest in her family concerns. He snapped his fingers and a waiter materialised with the bill. It was always the same. Where waiters were concerned, Adrian attracted first-class service while she was invisible.

As they were leaving the restaurant, Jessie noticed the time. 'Oh, my, I'll have to hurry home. Jo is dropping Sam back in half an hour.'

The temperature in the car dropped by several degrees. 'You still let him see the child?'

'Sam stays with Jo when I have to travel on business,' she said, sticking to the literal truth.

'How civilised.'

She couldn't let him think badly of Jo, who'd been her lifeline through the years since he had left. 'Sam loves Jo. And he's a playmate to Nell, who's the same age. They missed each other badly when Jo moved out.'

Adrian kept his eyes fixed on the winding road ahead, his face moving in and out of shadow as they drove under a canopy of trees whose branches linked up overhead. The shifting shadows made him look like a Greek statue, and just as unreachable. 'How old is Sam, Jessica?' he asked quietly.

She answered automatically, not even sensing the trap, 'He's six, seven in March.'

With a screech of tyres, the powerful car crossed the yellow centre line, before he wrenched it back under control. 'You bitch,' he swore under his breath. Stepping on the brake, he brought the car to a shuddering stop in a clearing, and slewed around to face her. There was fire in his eyes. 'It was staring me in the face all along and I couldn't see it, or didn't want to.'

Recoiling from his anger, she found the cold metal of the door at her back. 'What on earth are you talking about?'

'You convinced me that you left because of me. But my adventuring was just a way to pin the blame on someone else, wasn't it?'

Her fingers raked through her hair—spiking it— as she fought to understand. 'What blame? I left because I couldn't stand waiting to hear that you'd killed yourself. Why should I feel guilty over it?'

'Because while I was fighting my way down the Jardine River, you were making conquests of your own—with Joe. Weren't you?'

Her fingers rammed against her mouth. 'Oh, my God!'

'The truth will out, Jessica,' he continued relentlessly. 'You knew you were having this man's child when you left. The two of you must have been overjoyed when I disappeared, leaving the field clear for you.'

The news had almost destroyed her, but there was no way she could make him believe her without revealing that Sam was his child. 'Take me home, please,' she said, in a dead monotone.

'Sure, home to Joe. It will be my pleasure. But not before I give him a taste of his own medicine.'

In shock, Jessie saw him unsnap his seatbelt and slide across the seat towards her. The doors were centrally locked so there was nowhere to go. She could only hold him at bay with words. 'Adrian, you don't want me now. Not after what you say I did.'

'Oh, I want you all right. You're the only woman I ever wanted. Even in the jungle when I was surrounded by temptation, I told myself it would be wrong to give in. Hell, you're still technically my wife. It meant something to me, even if it didn't to you.'

'I was always faithful to you,' she defended herself.

The mocking gleam was rekindled in his gaze as he loomed over her. 'Always? What about Sam?'

'Is this what you learned in the jungle?' she said, her voice lifting with alarm. She didn't want him to take her in his arms..heaven forbid, to kiss her. All the good she had done, making a life where she didn't have to torment herself with what was happening to him, would be undone. She would be right back where she started, loving him hopelessly, pointlessly. Except that now he hated her for what he thought she had done.

His fingers nudged the edges of her winged collar and travelled around the back of her neck. The pressure wasn't enough to move her head, but she found herself inclining towards him, her face up-tilted and her lips parted at the mere thought of his kiss.

'This isn't jungle law, this is Adrian's law,' he murmured. 'This law says that what's mine stays mine.' His head turned fractionally, bringing their mouths into alignment. Swiftly, he claimed her, as she had known he would.

The six years between them fell away as if they had never been. She was his eager bride again, her veil tossed back over sun-brown hair, so that he could claim his first kiss as her husband.

His lips moved sensuously over hers, his touch feather-light and teasing, daring her to open to him. When she did, he deepened the kiss, drawing her closer until she felt the hardness of his body through the silken gown. The promise of their wedding night was rich in his kiss and excitement thrilled through her. She kissed him back with all her heart and soul.

'You should have been an actress,' he growled suddenly.

Horrified, she pulled away as the dream vanished abruptly. 'You bastard!'

'A word you are no doubt familiar with,' Adrian said, unperturbed by her fury.

She wanted to spit and claw her way out of his car. 'You're the one who's changed,' she hissed. It was an effort to force the sound out. Her throat felt tight with the words she dared not say and the tears she wouldn't give him the satisfaction of shedding. 'You were once caring and kind. Now...'

'Now I find I've been harbouring a beautiful illusion,' he said, shifting back to his side of the car. He stared out at the scenery, breathing deeply as if to regain control of himself. 'In the jungle, I almost convinced myself you were right—that I should have considered your feelings before rushing off to the ends of the earth. Damn it, it wouldn't have made any difference, would it?'

She scrubbed a hand across her mouth as if to wipe away the bitter-sweet taste of his kiss. He saw the gesture and frowned. 'Don't pretend you didn't enjoy it. I felt the truth in every nerve of your body.'

'All right, I enjoyed it,' she threw at him, anger slowly replacing her despair. What right had he to judge her, when he was the one risking his life on one *Boy's Own* quest after another?

In dismay, she realised she was letting herself believe the unsavoury picture he painted of her. 'Are you satisfied now?' she demanded with more irony than he knew.

He gunned the motor with a savage gesture, and the tyres bit into gravel as he swung the car back on to the road. 'I'm satisfied,' he said at last. 'The way you responded to me just now was very satisfying indeed. At least now I know that whenever you're with this Joe character you'll be thinking of how it could have been with us.'

Adrian didn't know it, but it was already that way. His kiss had only served to renew his hold over her. Would she ever be free of it?

'I'm glad I've finally done something to make you happy,' Jessie said, as bitterness welled up inside her. 'It isn't enough to stop you walling me off, I suppose?'

His impatient sigh hissed between them. 'The wall has nothing to do with you. I've been hounded by the media ever since I got back. If I'm to get any work done, I need the wall to give me some peace and privacy.'

'So there's no way I can make you change your mind?'

Adrian swore under his breath. 'You don't give up, do you? Actually, there is a way.'

She knew better than to allow herself to hope. 'What is it?'

'You could sell your place to me. I'd pay you enough so you could buy something decent elsewhere.'

As far away from him as possible, she supposed. The idea was tempting. It would free her from the torment of seeing him daily, knowing what he thought of her, and being unable to do anything to change it.

And there was Sam. Despite the risk that Adrian could stumble on the secret of Sam's parentage, she had her son's welfare to consider. 'I can't sell,' she said reluctantly, 'I had a hard enough time finding the right school for Sam as it was.'

'I never thought of you as a school snob,' Adrian remarked.

'I'm not. I told you he's ususually bright. That isn't my opinion—he's been tested several times,' she added, before he accused her of excessive maternal pride.

'So what's the problem?'

'Very few schools are equipped to cope with children as bright as Sam. Where he was before, he wasn't sufficiently challenged. Out of boredom, he started playing up.'

'There were behavioural difficulties?'

'Major ones.' Jessie thought back to the traumas and tantrums of the year before. 'I can't risk uprooting him now.'

'I can understand that.' Adrian's tone was surprisingly civil.

'Then you see why I don't want to sell up and move?'

'Of course. So you'd better learn to like my wall.'

# CHAPTER THREE

Jo HELPED herself to another chocolate biscuit. Watching her, Jessie was momentarily jealous. How could anyone eat as much as Jo did and not put on an ounce of weight? Her friend was a shade over five feet tall with the figure of a ballet dancer, which she had been in her teens before she became a music teacher. She still walked like a dancer, her movements graceful and loose-limbed. She also possessed one of the kindest hearts in Adelaide.

'I tried to tell you but you wouldn't listen,' she said around a mouthful of biscuit.

'I was asleep on my feet. Besides, I never dreamed you were trying to warn me about the wall.'

'Not the wall, its owner. When you mentioned seeing Adrian I thought I was too late, but you convinced yourself that he was an illusion, conjured out of your jet lag. I nearly had heart failure when I saw the two of you drive up.'

Jessie grimaced. 'How was I to know it was really Adrian? I must have been the only person in South Australia who didn't know he was back.'

'It made quite a splash for a few days,' Jo agreed, 'but either it didn't reach California, or you were too busy to read the newspapers. I thought I'd have plenty of time to warn you before you ran into him——' she screwed up her face '—and I would have done if you'd had the decency to sleep until

41

I brought Sam back. You promised,' she added, sounding aggrieved.

Jessie threw up her hands. 'Believe me, I tried. But it's hard to sleep when your garden is doubling as a construction site.'

Jo listened for a moment but the only sound was of their offspring playing together in the garden. 'They aren't working today?'

'The builder said they wouldn't be back for a few days, but somehow, I don't think it's because I objected.'

There was the sound of a tennis ball smacking against brick. 'At least the children have found a use for the wall, even if it isn't the one the owner intended.'

'I'm glad someone's getting pleasure out of it.' She shot her friend a look of appeal. 'What am I going to do, Jo? I can't just sit here while he walls me in. The garden's like a prison already and there's still one whole side to be built.'

'You've tried reasoning with your ex-husband?'

Technically, he was anything but 'ex', but Jessie let it pass. 'I did everything short of going down on my knees to him. But he's changed since he went away. He's harder and colder. No amount of reasoning reaches him.'

She had already explained to Jo where Adrian had been and why he had allowed the world to believe he was dead. Jo nodded sagely. 'It isn't what you want to hear, love, but maybe you had something to do with the change.'

'Me? How could I?'

'If he loves you, the break-up probably hurt him a lot.'

Jessie dismissed this possibility with a flick of her fingers. 'I'd agree with you *if* he really loved me. But I was another challenge: once he conquered me, he was ready to move on to the next challenge.'

Jo gestured with her coffee-cup. 'At least it wasn't another woman.'

'I almost wish it had been. You can't scratch the eyes out of a mountain.'

'You've got a point there.' Jo's expression was anxious as she looked out of the window at the two children at play. 'Have you thought of selling up and moving away?'

Jessie sighed. 'Adrian even offered to buy me out. It would solve a lot of problems, but it would create just as many new ones. I couldn't handle another year like the last one with Sam.'

'You could come and live with me,' Jo suggested. 'I drive to school every day. It wouldn't be far out of my way to drop Sam off.'

Jessie wanted to hug her. 'What would I do without you, Jo Napier?' she said in a choked voice. 'But you and Chris haven't been married long enough to cope with interlopers.'

'Nonsense. Chris knows how I feel about you and Sam. And Nell misses Sam a lot.'

'He misses her, too,' Jessie agreed. 'But running away isn't the answer. As long as Adrian and I are in the same city, the difficulties remain.'

Jo's blue eyes regarded her over the rim of her cup. 'Are you still in love with him?'

Despair gripped Jessie. 'I wish I knew. I know I did the only thing I could in leaving him. Remembering those times, waiting for news of him—I couldn't go through it again. Believing he was dead made it easier—I could grieve for him and get over it. Now...'

'Now, the only difference is he's alive. It's not a second coming,' Jo said gently.

Jessie turned moist eyes to her. 'But it could be a second chance.'

Jo muttered savagely under her breath. 'Men! Why do we let ourselves love the ones who can hurt us the most?'

'Was it the same for you and Thorne?'

Jo nodded. 'At times, I wanted to murder him for working in such a dangerous profession. But I took him on "till death us do part".'

'Surely they had natural causes in mind when they wrote that part?'

Jo's bright gaze locked with hers. 'I'm not so sure. I don't recall seeing any footnotes in the marriage ceremony.'

'Are you saying I should have stayed with Adrian no matter what?'

With a sigh, Jo set her cup down. 'Only you know the answer, my friend.'

She seemed about to leave and a feeling of panic assailed Jessie. 'Before you go, there's something I must ask you.'

'Anything. What is it?'

Jessie swallowed hard. 'If you run into Adrian, please don't tell him that you're the Jo I was living with while he was gone.'

A self-deprecating grin tilted up the corners of Jo's mouth. 'I knew it, you're ashamed of me.'

Jessie looked stricken until she saw that Jo was teasing her. 'I'm nothing of the sort. But when I mentioned you, Adrian jumped to the conclusion that you're a man. He thinks Joe is the name of Sam's father.'

A soft whistle punctuated Jo's response. 'Why would you let him think so, for heaven's sake?'

'I can't tell him the truth. You don't know Adrian. He's an all-or-nothing man. If he finds out that Sam is his son he'll move heaven and earth to get custody of him.'

Jo frowned. 'Is it so wrong for Adrian to have access to his son?'

'I'd give anything for Sam to get to know his father. But there's no way Adrian will settle for being a weekend parent.'

Jessie saw her own pain mirrored in her friend's expression. 'Now I understand. But could he get custody when he didn't even know Sam existed until now? You're the only parent Sam's ever known. Judges aren't monsters.'

'I know, but I daren't take the risk. Raising Sam by myself must weigh in my favour, but there was all that trouble at school last year. It might look as if I let my work interfere with my duties as a parent.'

No doubt remembering the times when she'd minded Sam while Jessie was away on business, Jo looked troubled. 'It could be twisted out of proportion if someone had a good enough reason to want to hurt you.'

The words slid out between parched lips. 'Adrian has a good enough reason. He hates me.'

'Does he know you're about to be unemployed?'

Jessie looked away, her silence more eloquent than words. 'Not yet, but he's bound to find out soon. I almost wish I hadn't been so noble in refusing to sign a new contract with Grattons.'

A violent shake of her head was Jo's answer. 'How could you? The hours they wanted you to work—not to mention the extra travelling—would be disastrous for you and Sam.'

'Being unemployed could be worse.' Jessie's eyes became huge with uncertainty. 'Oh, Jo, I planned everything so carefully, researching stores in California like the one I want to open. Now I don't know whether to go through with my plans, or go back to Grattons and eat humble pie.'

Her friend paced back and forth behind the couch. 'It's a rotten situation, either way. I don't suppose you've thought about going back to Adrian?'

Mechanically, Jessie began to gather up the coffee things. 'What makes you think he'd want me back?'

'You say he hates you. But isn't it because he thinks you had an affair and got pregnant while you were still together? If he knows that Sam is his son, he has no reason to hate you.'

Jessie's fingers tightened around the tray and the cups rattled as a tremor shook her. 'I can't go back for the same reason I left in the first place. I'd never have a moment's peace for worrying about him. Sam's better off without a father than learning to love Adrian only to lose him.'

There was an expression of longing in Jo's pale blue eyes as she went to the window and looked out at the playing children. 'I wonder if Nell would agree with you.'

Jessie touched her friend's arm. 'I'm sorry, Jo. I didn't think what I was saying.'

Jo pulled herself together with a visible effort. 'It's OK. She has Chris now and she already looks on him as her father.'

Impulsively, Jessie hugged her. 'I'm so happy for you all.'

Returning the pressure, Jo smiled. 'Thanks.' She held Jessie at arm's length and looked serious. 'Here's an idea. What if you went to see Sir Mark Gratton? You were always good friends and you know this latest stunt was well meant.'

'But he doesn't have anything to do with the store now.'

'I know, but he's bound to have influential friends who do. Maybe he could help you to negotiate a better contract.'

Why hadn't she thought of it? She gripped Jo more tightly. 'You're a genius. It's worth a try, at least. And I do want to see their new home.'

When Jessie rang her, Lady Gratton was equally anxious to show it off. 'We wondered how you were getting on,' she said, when Jessie identified herself on the telephone.

'I need to talk to you about that,' Jessie began.

But Susan forestalled her. 'Let's not talk now. Come to tea tomorrow. Mark will be delighted to see you.'

Would he now? Jessie thought, as she replaced the receiver. She had no doubt that Susan was the one behind the surprise they'd sprung on her, and wondered if Sir Mark had approved.

The question was settled as soon as she arrived at their new home the next day. After being shown around the luxurious retirement villa—set in its own grounds, but with access to an amazing array of

facilities from croquet to a heated spa pool—she
was shown into a spacious living-room where afternoon tea was set out.

While Susan poured the tea, Sir Mark took both
of Jessie's hands in his gnarled ones. 'Tell me dear,
have you forgiven my wife for meddling in your
affairs?' Susan kept her eyes on the tea-tray, but
she tensed visibly.

'There's nothing to forgive, I know you meant
well,' Jessie said, and she saw Susan relax slightly.
'I just wish you'd told me what you had in mind,'
she couldn't help adding.

When she looked up, Susan's eyes were misty. 'It
seemed so perfect, Adrian coming back just when
we were ready to part with the house.'

'She's an incurable romantic,' Sir Mark said, but
the gaze he turned on his wife was filled with
affection.

'You may have to wait a while for a happy
ending,' Jessie said. 'I wasn't completely honest
with you about the break-up. Adrian and I aren't
on good terms.'

Alarm replaced Susan's dreamy expression. 'Oh,
dear, what have we done?'

Sir Mark's eyebrow lifted. '*We?* I wasn't the one
who insisted on packing and leaving with unseemly
haste.'

His wife wrung her hands. 'It's all my fault. I
only wanted Jessie and little Sam to be happy.'

Jessie knelt at her side and took her hand. 'We
*are* happy. Just the way we are.'

'Then you don't hate me for meddling in your
life?'

Emphatically, Jessie shook her head. 'I love you both. You're like family to me, and I know whatever you did was with the best of intentions.'

Sir Mark rattled his teacup noisily and his wife rushed to refill it. 'Now that's out of the way, what's this I hear about you leaving the store?'

'It's true, unfortunately. It hasn't been the same place since it changed hands.' She explained about the terms of her new contract, glad that he had given her such an easy opening. 'I wouldn't mind the extra hours if it weren't for Sam,' she concluded.

There was complete agreement in Sir Mark's expression. 'Why must people confuse the quantity of hours put in with the quality of the work put out? We pioneered flexible working hours and never had a complaint about service. Happy people perform better; don't they realise?'

As his voice rose in frustration, his wife put a hand on his arm. 'Don't upset yourself, dear. New brooms have to sweep in their own fashion.'

He gave a deep sigh. 'You're right, as usual. Still, they'll regret their sweeping if it loses them talents like young Jessie here.'

'I'm not sure I'm such a great loss,' she admitted, 'but I'll miss the job—which is what I want to ask you about.'

Sir Mark leaned forward. 'What is it, my dear?'

'I wondered if you could talk to someone at the store about my new contract. If I could keep to my present terms of employment, I wouldn't have to leave.'

He stroked his chin thoughtfully. 'I haven't much influence there any more, since I turned down a seat on the board. But I will try.'

Jessie flung her arms around him. 'You're an angel.'

He winked at her. 'That's not what Susan calls me.'

'Old devil is more like it,' his wife confirmed but with warmth in her voice. 'What will you do if the contract can't be sorted out?' she asked Jessie.

'I hope to go into business for myself,' she confessed somewhat shyly. Their supportive expressions encouraged her to go on. 'A man I work with at the store—Joseph Reiner—is also leaving and we want to start a budget decorating service together, working out of a shop-front.'

'It sounds promising,' Sir Mark murmured, 'especially the budget angle.'

'Most people think of decorators as expensive,' Susan agreed.

'We thought we should advertise fixed prices for all our services,' Jessie went on, her voice vibrant with enthusiasm. 'People will know exactly how much they're up for at each stage. They can stop at any time, or have us do the complete job. The only extras are the materials, and we'll have various price groupings for those, too.'

Sir Mark looked thoughtful. 'Do you have premises in mind?'

'Not yet. I intend to look around now I've finished my last commission for the store.'

'A friend of mine—a property developer—has a new shopping mall opening in a few weeks. Your business would be an ideal tenant. If you like, I'll recommend you to him—if the contract thing doesn't work out.'

A thrill of anticipation surged through her. She could hardly wait to tell Joseph that one of their major problems might already be solved. 'I don't know how to thank you,' she said sincerely.

'You could bring that brilliant son of yours to visit us,' Susan suggested.

Jessie laughed. 'It's a promise.'

Her brilliant son wasn't playing in the garden when she got home. And the babysitter's car wasn't parked in its usual place in front of the house. Instantly, panic surged through her. Had something happened to Sam? Visions of the babysitter racing him off to hospital filled her mind. Maybe the woman had tried to call her while she was driving home from the Grattons' place.

'Dolores? Sam?' Her voice rose with fear as she tore inside, shedding her things in the hall as she went.

A shrill cry ripped from her throat as she cannoned into a hard, masculine body. Strong arms encircled her, steadying her. 'Easy, Jessica. It's only me.'

Wild-eyed, she twisted in his grasp. 'Adrian, what are you doing here? Has something happened to Sam?'

'Hey, take it easy. Nothing's happened. He's safe here, with me.'

She had to see for herself. Pushing his hands away, she rocketed into the living-room, coming up short at the sight of her son sitting on the floor amid of sea of paper shapes and diagrams. He barely looked up. 'Hi, Mum.'

'Hi, yourself.' She had to force the words out while her eyes feasted on the sight of him, well and whole, not twisted and broken as she'd feared. Nausea overwhelmed her and she slumped against the door-frame.

She sensed Adrian's approach. 'Are you all right?'

'I will be in a minute. When I came home and found you, I thought . . .'

'The worst, I know. My mother was the same when I started rock-climbing in my teens. I guess it goes with a mother's job.' He smiled crookedly. 'But as you can see, he's fine.'

Anger seeped in to replace her fear. 'So I see. Would you mind telling me what this is all about? Where's Dolores?'

'Let me get you some tea, then I'll tell you the whole story. The kettle's already boiled. It won't take a minute.'

By the time his minute was up and he'd returned with the tea, Jessie's fury had reached boiling point. How dared he dismiss her fears and those of his mother, waiting for news of him? He didn't know the thousand deaths every mother died when a child was endangered. How could he? He didn't stay in one place long enough to generate that much loyalty to another person.

'You're angry with me,' Adrian said, catching sight of her set expression.

'You're dead right I am. And the explanation better be good.'

'Now just a minute. I'm not on trial here, so you can drop the holier-than-thou tone of voice. As it happens, I did you a favour.'

'What favour?'

'Your babysitter got a telephone call to say that her own child had been injured at a Boy Scout meeting. They were waiting for her at some hospital, needing her signature before they could operate.'

Her hand went to her throat. 'Dear heaven! Will he be all right?' Like herself, Dolores Baxter was a single parent. Her son, Daniel, was all she had.

'They think so, but she had to get to him right away. She tried to reach you by phone but you were on your way back here. I met her at the gate, just about hysterical, and volunteered to sit with Sam until you got back. That photo of the two of us—in the back of one of my books—convinced her that I was really your husband. Even in the state she was in, she wouldn't turn Sam over to a stranger.'

Suddenly she felt very small. 'I owe you an apology,' she admitted. 'Thank you for stepping in to help.'

Her anger had left its mark, she noted, in the coldness of his tone and the tense set of his mouth. His expression softened, however, as he looked at Sam, playing on the floor. 'It was no trouble. Sam and I got along just fine.'

Hearing his name, the child looked up. 'Did you know that Dr Cole is a meteorologist? He can forecast the weather,' he explained, his six-year-old features bright with excitement at the discovery.

She ruffled his hair. 'Yes, I know he can forecast the weather.' He could do a lot of other things, like hold her soul captive and set her body aflame with need of him, she remembered. She doubted whether Sam would be impressed by those qualifications.

In that respect, he was a normal six-year-old, dismissing all forms of male-female interaction as 'yucky'.

'Sam and I were discussing the weather,' Adrian said solemnly.

Sam's eyes gleamed. 'Do you know that we live at the bottom of an ocean of air?' he asked. 'It's called the at-mos-phere.'

'How about that?' She pretended wide-eyed astonishment. 'Why don't we drown in this ocean?'

Sam's nose wrinkled in disgust at her ignorance. 'Because it's made of air, of course. Weather is the swirling movement of the air in the bit nearest us.'

'Which is called...' Adrian prompted.

'The trop...troposphere,' Sam stated, grinning with pride.

Glancing at the diagrams which she now saw represented the movement of air masses over the continents, Jessie smiled. 'You two have been busy.'

Adrian shrugged. 'I had to do something to keep him occupied, and Lego lasted about five minutes.'

Keeping Sam's active brain interested and challenged was a problem she knew only too well. In a short time, Adrian had found the key, which was to stretch his young mind as far as it was able, and a little beyond. Learning new things was Sam's favourite hobby.

Taking a deep breath, she offered her hand to Adrian. 'Will you forgive me for jumping to conclusions? I appreciate what you did for Sam and Dolores Baxter.'

He touched his palm to hers, the warm dry feel of it sending an electric charge along her arm so that she jerked back in surprise. His touch had always held a special magic for her, but she had counted on time and distance to insulate her. However, she was tired and vulnerable, still shaky from her fears for Sam. It had to be the explanation.

Her instinctive response brought an angry glitter to his eyes. 'Do you have to jump when I touch you? How do you think it makes me feel?'

Aiming a warning frown in Sam's direction, she lowered her voice. 'How you feel is all that matters, as usual. My feelings don't come into it, when you insist on building your own private Jericho out there, for instance.'

'If you must know, the wall is at a standstill,' he informed her. 'The builder can't match the handmade bricks.'

She clapped her hands silently together. 'I'll rush out and get a suntan while I still can.'

He looked as if he was about to explode. 'Damn it, I thought you'd be pleased. It could be weeks before they locate another shipment of the same bricks.'

The victory, temporary though it was, should have delighted her. Instead, she felt deflated, as if she had lost instead of won. It occurred to her that she was disappointed. She had wanted him to give up the wall for her sake, not because of a shortage of materials. Why it made a difference, she couldn't say. She only knew that it did.

'I'd be a hypocrite not to be pleased,' she acknowledged. 'But I'm sorry you're having problems.'

He gave her a grudging smile. 'Thanks. Actually, the whole business of civilisation is a bit much to cope with again. In the jungle, you live on a knife-edge but at least you can fight to survive. How do you fight tradesmen and bureaucrats?'

Her smile was genuine this time. 'Welcome back to the real world.'

Sam brought a piece of paper to Adrian and tugged at his arm. 'Tell me again which are the horse latitudes.'

The diagram showed the world divided into bands from north to south. He stabbed at a band across the centre. 'This is the thundery zone of rising air, remember? Above and below it are the horse latitudes of calm, sinking air.'

Her eyebrow lifted. 'The horse latitudes?'

'In the olden days, the people travelling in ships in that part had to throw their horses overboard to save water,' Sam told her importantly.

Accustomed to her son coming out with some astonishing titbit of information, Jessie barely blinked. 'I see. And what does all this tell you?'

Sam's brows drew together in concentration. 'It's like a battleground, where the air masses and the jet streams meet and cause changes in our weather.'

'Very good. Next time, I'll tell you all about air pressure,' Adrian promised him.

Sam's eyes shone. 'I'm going to be a meteorologist like you, Dr Cole.' Then he turned to Jessie. 'Did you know that Dr Cole's been to the top of Mount Everest and all the way to the South Pole?'

His enthusiasm was so infectious that she had to laugh. 'Yes, darling, and he's been to lots of other places besides. I'm sure he'll tell you about them if you don't make a pest of yourself.'

'I'm not a pest, am I, Dr Cole?' Sam demanded indignantly.

Adrian ruffled the child's hair and a pang shot through Jessie. Sam was already halfway in love with Adrian. Was it fair to keep them apart? She hardened her heart. Knowing Adrian, she couldn't risk it. 'All the same, you'd better say goodnight to Dr Cole. I'm sure he has lots of things he wants to do besides talk to you.'

Sam looked at Adrian. 'Have you asked her yet?'

'No, not yet. Perhaps you should ask her.'

Fingers of ice clutched at her heart. What was going on between them? Did Adrian already suspect the truth? The suspense was almost unbearable.

'Dr Cole said he would show me photographs of his expeditions, if you say it's all right,' Sam informed her. Then he did one of his little-boy transformations. 'Can we, Mum, please? Can we?'

How could she deny him anything? Besides, it was probably one of those polite invitations which didn't mean anything. 'I don't see any harm in it.'

'Great. How about tonight?' Adrian suggested.

A lump rose in her throat. 'We've already taken up too much of your time.'

'My time is my own. I'll happily send out for some food so you can relax. You look as if you could use the break.'

'Please, Mum?'

She felt as if she was under siege from the two of them. The idea of spending the evening with Adrian daunted her. Already she was alarmingly aware of her responses to him, which, far from being diminished by their separation, seemed to be stronger than ever.

Flashes of their life together kept intruding on her thoughts, stirring sensations inside her which she had believed dead and buried.

And there was Sam to consider. His teachers said he suffered from a lack of male influence in his life. Seeing him with Adrian, it seemed possible. She had rarely seen him so animated. And he had a right to know his father, even if he didn't know their real relationship.

She had a horrible feeling she was going to regret this. 'Very well, we'll come,' she conceded. Sam and Adrian had identical expressions of triumph on their faces. The sight gave her a cold feeling of dread, as if sides had already been chosen.

# CHAPTER FOUR

'WHO is this Auntie Drew Sam keeps quoting?' Adrian asked, as they walked back to his house.

Jessie said a prayer of thanks for old habits. She hadn't counted on Adrian meeting Sam so soon. In his innocence, Sam could have given the whole game away. 'Auntie Drew is Mrs Drury, a friend who helped me when he was born,' she informed Adrian. 'As a baby, Sam couldn't get his tongue around Drury. She's Mrs Napier now but she'll probably be Auntie Drew forever.'

There was a distant roll of thunder and wet splotches dropped on to her face. 'It looks like we're in for a storm.'

'I noticed it building up. We'd better hurry or we'll get soaked.' He picked Sam up in one strong arm and dropped the other around her shoulders, sheltering her with his body. Nevertheless, they were all thoroughly damp by the time they dashed under his portico.

'Sam's shivering. He needs a hot bath,' Adrian said, when they were safely inside. Outside, the storm had built up to a howling fury.

Conscious of the cocooning effect of the storm, which isolated them like shipwreck victims on a desert island, she shook her head. 'He also needs a change of clothes. We should go home before this gets any worse.'

'It's already worse. I'll find something dry for him to wear while you run the bath.'

There was little she could do but comply. From visits to the Grattons, she knew her way around the big old house and Sam was soon splashing in the deep claw-footed tub. Adrian came in with a T-shirt screen-printed in an African design with the word 'Zimbabwe' across it. 'Think he'd like to wear this?'

'It'll reach his knees, but he'll adore it.' She draped the shirt over a towel rail and perched on the edge of the bath, squeezing spongefuls of warm water down her son's back. He squirmed happily.

'Portrait of the Madonna and child,' Adrian observed.

Her face took on a glow which she blamed on the steam. She refused to think it was because his remark pleased her. She wished he would find something else to do. His penetrating gaze scorched her, although her back was half-turned to him. 'I can manage now, thanks,' she said with a touch of asperity.

The obvious dismissal brought a frown to his features. 'Very well. I've sent out for Chinese food.'

'In this weather?' She was surprised that he had remembered her preference in take-away food.

'Not rain, nor snow, nor dark of night...' he said with an ironic smile. 'It should be here by the time you've finished your bath.'

Jessie *was* damp from the rain, but taking a bath in his house suggested an intimacy for which she was unprepared. 'I don't need one. My clothes are almost dry,' she assured him, nervousness threading her voice with tension.

He ran a hand down her back and a shudder rippled through her. 'This is soaked. You'll catch cold.'

He disappeared and returned with a fluffy white terry towelling bathrobe. 'This should do until your clothes are dry.'

He insisted on helping her to dry Sam, then took him off to the living-room while she had her bath. In Adrian's T-shirt, Sam looked like an urchin— an Oliver Twist with thin brown legs sticking out from the knee-length garment. He wore it proudly and read the African name aloud, pressing Adrian for details of its origin. The lesson in African sociology faded away down the hall as she replaced the plug in the tub and turned on the water.

There was a jar of bath-salts beside the tub and she tipped some into the water, where they made a collar of foam. With a blissful sigh, she slid under the foam until only her head and shoulders protruded.

In the distance, Sam's voice, high and piping, alternated with Adrian's deep one. Although she couldn't discern the words, the sound reassured her. It was easy to fantasise that they were a real family. The storm raging outside compounded the illusion of cosy familiarity. If Adrian had only settled down, this could be the reality.

'I knocked but you didn't hear me. I brought you some champagne.'

Her head snapped up as he came into the room and stood a glass on the edge of the bath. Daydreaming, she hadn't heard the voices stop. Her skin tingled with awareness of him and she strove for equanimity. 'Thank you. I'll enjoy it.'

Instead of leaving, he leaned against the wall as if he intended to watch her drink the champagne. Her hand shook as she picked up the glass and held it to her lips. Maybe if she drank it quickly, he would leave.

'Take your time, the food won't be here for another fifteen minutes,' he said with maddening calm. Evidently the sight of her in the bath didn't affect him any more. The thought was unaccountably depressing.

'What's Sam doing?' she asked.

'Looking at photos of my trip to the South Pole.' Adrian glanced away, his expression distant. 'He's a wonderful boy, Jessica.'

The implication was clear. He didn't blame the son for the sins of his mother. 'I'm proud of him,' she said defensively.

He nodded. 'With good reason. In personality, he reminds me of myself at the same age. It's almost uncanny.'

The stem of the champagne glass seemed to crumble in her hand and shards of glass showered the tiles and the surface of the water.

Adrian reacted quickly. 'Don't move, you'll cut yourself to ribbons.' He spread several towels across the shards, their thickness protecting her feet as he helped her out of the water and swathed her in another towel. In an automatic gesture he pushed the damp strands of hair away from her forehead. As their eyes locked, Jessie felt the colour leave her face.

'Jessica.' He said her name like a caress, his voice hoarse and deep. Swaddled in towels, she was helpless when he put his arms around her. 'This is just like old times, isn't it?'

Her tongue darted out to moisten her lips and he caught his breath. 'I don't . . .' she began, not sure what it was she didn't.

'Mum, the delivery man's at the door.' The spell shattered as Sam's voice floated along the hall.

Adrian's expression hardened at the reminder of what he thought was her faithlessness. 'I'll go. Be careful of the glass as you dry yourself.'

A few cuts seemed insignificant compared to the pain which sliced through her as he went out. Like old times, he had said. For a moment, she had erased the pain and loneliness of the last years, responding to his touch as if they still belonged together.

It took Sam to remind her that it was an illusion. Adrian had never belonged to her in any way which mattered, or she would never have left. She resolved to keep it in mind.

Under Adrian's direction, Sam was tipping Chinese food into serving dishes when she joined them. Adrian's glance took in the robe belted tightly around her waist, and her hair turbanned in another towel. She tensed, waiting for a sign that the magic hadn't completely gone, but she might as well have been fully dressed for all the response he showed.

'Dinner's almost ready,' he announced. To Sam, he added, 'Chopsticks or cutlery?'

'Chopsticks, please. Mum showed me how to use them.'

A mocking smile curved his lips. 'Your mother is full of surprises.'

A pulse hammered at her throat. 'I had a good teacher.'

She meant him but he chose to misunderstand. 'The famous Joe?'

Innocently, Sam piped in, 'Auntie Drew says chopsticks are a good way to eat less. She eats lasagne with them.' He giggled.

The change of subject disconcerted Adrian, who didn't know that Sam automatically connected any mention of Joe with his Auntie Drew, the only Jo he knew. 'I suppose it's one way to lose weight,' he said distractedly.

He put a bowl and chopsticks in front of her, but Jessie's appetite had gone. She pushed some chow mein around the plate, eating little. It was a relief when Sam polished off the last of his spring rolls and announced that he was full.

She pushed her chair away from the table. 'In that case, I'd better get you home to bed, young man.'

Sam's face contorted in protest. 'Aw, Mum.'

'I think you should sleep here,' Adrian said.

Surprise almost made her snap a chopstick in half. 'Now just a minute...'

His face was impassive, as if he hadn't just suggested that she sleep with him. At least, she *thought* that was what he was suggesting. Maybe the champagne had been a deliberate ploy to break down her reserves.

'You can't take him home in this,' he said, shattering any such notion.

Her awareness had been so centred on him that she almost forgot the storm raging outside. Its fury had doubled since they arrived. She didn't enjoy the idea of another soaking. 'It's all your fault,' she muttered.

Adrian's eyebrows tilted and annoyance gleamed in his eyes. 'So now the weather is my fault, too?'

'I didn't mean the weather. If it weren't for your blasted wall, we could take a short cut across the garden instead of having to go home the long way.'

Adrian's fingers clenched so tightly that his knuckles whitened. 'Susan Gratton has a lot to answer for.'

Surprise rippled through Jessie as she allowed herself to consider that he might be less than thrilled with their situation. Like her, he was a victim of Susan's machinations and probably didn't like it any more than Jessica did. 'You're right,' she said in a forgiving tone. 'If you'd had an ordinary neighbour instead of me, the wall would have been perfectly reasonable.'

Sam yawned hugely and Jessie glanced at Adrian, wondering what she ought to do. He solved the problem by hefting the child into his arms. 'Come on, Sam, bedtime.'

The child giggled and linked his arms around Adrian's neck. Jessie experienced a recurrence of the feeling that it was two against one. In troubled silence, she followed Adrian down the hall and into a small side bedroom. She was surprised to see a single bed already turned down.

'I made it up while you were in the bath, just in case,' Adrian explained.

A spark of indignation flared inside her, then was quickly extinguished. She had to stop taking everything he said so personally. She reached to take Sam from his arms, and the boy gave her a heavy-lidded smile. 'He's nearly asleep already.'

Sam scrubbed his eyes with doubled fists. 'I'm not tired.' Another yawn gave the lie to his assertion.

Laughter replaced her irritation. 'So I see.'

Adrian hovered nearby while Jessie tucked Sam under the covers. By the time she dropped a kiss on to his brow, his eyes were closed. 'This is when he looks like a six-year-old,' she said, standing back.

Adrian's hand rested on her shoulder. 'The rest of the time, he's six going on sixteen.' He snapped the light off. In companionable silence they watched the sleeping child, his face illuminated in a shaft of brilliance from the hall; then they backed quietly out of the room.

Halfway down the hall, they were suddenly plunged into darkness. Jessie let out an involuntary shriek.

She felt the warmth of Adrian's hand against her back. 'Relax, it's only a power cut.'

Terrific! All she needed now was a candle-lit evening with him. Were the elements conspiring against her peace of mind now?

He guided her back to the living-room and lit a pair of decorative candles standing on a sideboard. 'Luckily David hasn't started on this room yet,' he observed. 'It's the only room besides the kitchen where I can still find anything.'

'The library's well advanced. I noticed it when we came in.' She was thankful to be on neutral ground, finding herself far too aware of him in the shadowed surroundings.

'There was only a section of the original timber wainscoting left but I'm having it copied so the room can be restored to its original splendour.'

'It should look wonderful,' she agreed. 'It's a pity so much of the land was sold off, otherwise you could rebuild the orchards and the English garden.'

'You know about them?' He sounded surprised.

'I did some research after I bought the gatehouse. In the late 1800s, the whole valley belonged to the house. Fruit from the cherry orchards was packed in cork dust and sent to Covent Garden in London. Carriage-loads of visitors came to see the English garden and orchid collection. Last century, the glasshouses contained some of the rarest plants in the world. Luckily, the original owner had his own gold mine, so he could afford the best plant stock available.'

Adrian went to the sideboard and poured wine from a decanter, then handed her a glass. 'Have you researched the house as well?'

'It was the property's farmhouse, built in the Georgian period. Why?'

'Just wondered.'

He sipped his wine in thoughtful silence which was punctuated by the howl of the storm outside. Every now and then, rain dashed against the windows and the room was illuminated by lightning stabbing across the sky.

After each flash Jessie flinched, waiting for the inevitable thunderbolt. They were so loud that they shook the house. Unconsciously, she shifted along the couch, nearer to Adrian.

He noticed the movement. 'You still don't like thunderstorms?'

Her head dropped forward, although he couldn't see her expression in the flickering light. 'I never did. I'm glad Sam's asleep, otherwise I'd have to pretend to be brave.'

'It isn't pretence. You have more courage than you give yourself credit for.'

She shook her head in denial. 'I couldn't climb mountains and strike out across continents the way you do.'

'Did,' he corrected her. 'But there are other kinds of courage.'

'I'm not sure I follow.'

His eyes were inky as he looked at her, the expression in them unreadable. 'It took courage to strike out on your own, to have a child and bring him up alone. It's courage of a different kind.'

'It's necessity,' she amended. 'Someone once said that courage is doing what you're afraid to do.' Adrian's previous comment finally struck her and she stared at him. 'Why did you say that climbing mountains was something you did—past tense?'

He gave a throaty chuckle. 'I wondered when you'd bite. You always wanted me to settle down. You could say I've finally done it.'

He couldn't see her wide-eyed astonishment in the dim light, but it was there all the same. 'You? A stay-at-home? Since when?'

'Since spending six years in the jungle, coming to terms with what's important in life.'

She strove to quell the hope which rose unbidden inside her. If he had really changed, was there hope for them after all? 'What about the new TV series?' she asked warily.

'I'm merely the co-presenter, the front man who sits in the studio and links each episode together with appropriate commentary. It's like sports reporting,' he explained. 'You needn't compete in every sport to comment on them.'

Whether it was the effects of the wine, or the strangeness of the occasion, she wasn't sure. But she felt light-headed, suddenly. She had told Jo that Adrian's return could be a second chance. Maybe it was more prophetic than she realised.

'Won't you miss the hands-on experience?' she asked guardedly.

Was it her imagination or did his fingers tighten around the wine glass? 'Of course I'll miss it. But I'm thirty-two years old. It's time I made room on the mountain for someone younger.'

Fear clutched at her heart, and she searched his face for signs of some affliction he hadn't told her about. But Adrian's features were as sharply chiselled as ever, and his body was lean and hard under his knitted shirt. Still, she had to know. 'There's nothing wrong, is there?'

'With me? Good grief, no.' He tilted his head to one side, regarding her with an expression of cynical amusement. 'Do I detect a caring note all of a sudden?'

Stung by his obvious scepticism, she pressed her hands tightly together. Of course she cared. She had never stopped caring. But she couldn't convince him when he thought she had left him for another man, the father of her child.

'You must allow me a little nostalgia,' she said lightly. 'The storm, the wine . . . you said yourself it's like old times.'

Exactly when he closed the gap between them she wasn't sure, but suddenly he lifted the glass from her hands and set it down on the coffee-table. One arm slid from the back of the couch on to her shoulders and drew her against him, while the other spanned her waist so that she was held captive in the circle of his embrace.

'Adrian.' It was meant to come out as a protest but it sounded more like an invitation. He burrowed his head against the opening of the towelling robe and his lips moved across the silken surface of her breasts. When his fiery tongue touched her nipple, a bonfire of longing erupted inside her, a little volcano of explosive pleasure.

She had waited so long to feel like this again, realising in the dim recesses of her mind that it could only happen with Adrian. And if he really *had* changed . . .

But what if he hadn't? He had only been back a few weeks. What if the old wanderlust overtook him again? With a supreme effort, she ignored the clamouring ache inside her which demanded his fulfilment, and quenched the fires his touch had ignited deep in the centre of her being. She needed to be sure of him before she gave full rein to the needs crying out for satisfaction inside her.

'Don't, please.' This time her words carried much more conviction.

He tugged the edges of her robe together and moved away. His dark gaze mocked her as he totally misread the reason for her change of heart. 'I forgot, you have other priorities these days. Does Joe know that your husband has moved in next door to you?'

How could she avoid an outright lie? 'I didn't see any need to discuss it,' she attempted.

'So he doesn't know. Are you afraid it will shatter his trust in you?'

'There's no Joe in my life—not the way you mean,' she snapped, suddenly sick and tired of the whole charade. If it hadn't been vital to provide a fictitious father for Sam, she would have confessed there and then.

His hooded gaze searched her face. 'Sounds like a cry from the heart. Was he the one who left, Jessica? Are you finally getting a taste of your own medicine?'

'What does it matter either way? Unless it makes you happy to think I was left high and dry.'

'How could it? I wasn't the one who wanted us to part, remember?'

'So now it's all my fault.'

Adrian swore softly. 'I didn't say it was.' He stood up and began to pace like a caged beast, in and out of the shadows, as if they were bars. 'There's no point in dredging it up again. It's over and done with.'

For him, perhaps, but not for her. She hadn't counted on tonight awakening so many memories. There hadn't been a man for her since Adrian, and six years was a long time. She felt the lack as a yearning which gnawed at her like a hunger. Could he feel it, too, or had he found other outlets for his passions? He said he'd resisted temptation in the jungle. But what about now that he was back in civilisation? A stab of anguish accompanied the thought, catching her by surprise. All of a sudden, she felt murderous, but towards whom?

'Maybe we should stick to neutral topics. Like your television series,' she suggested. 'Does it have a name?'

'The working title is *Edge of Reality*. The producer wants to take people to places they've never seen before—the underground rivers of New Guinea and the Cape York escarpments—even out into space if we can line it up.'

Adrian's enthusiasm wasn't lost on her. Couldn't he hear himself? A moment ago, he had spoken about settling down, but it only took an innocent question to fire him up. How long would it be before he hounded the producer into letting him go along on an expedition?

Chilled by the thought, she was glad she hadn't let him kiss her. His touch was incendiary. If she wasn't careful, the flames could consume her.

Healing herself sufficiently to go on had been her personal Everest. Letting Adrian back into her life would be like starting again at the foot of the mountain. Still, it beckoned—oh, how it beckoned.

'It looks as if the power is off for the night,' Adrian said. He picked up a candle and handed it to her, then took the other one himself. 'We'd better turn in.'

The room he showed her to was the one Susan Gratton had kept for her goddaughter's visits. Adrian must have bought most of the furniture with the house, because she recognised the early colonial cedar bed with its high posts at each corner, and the antique dresser which Susan had rescued from a junk-shop. The room had been stripped back to bare floorboards and brick walls.

'Sorry it isn't more comfortable, but I didn't expect house guests,' he apologised.

'It's fine. Although I can't help thinking that Sam and I could be home in fifteen minutes.'

'And soaked to the skin because of my wall,' he said ruefully. 'Putting you up is the least I can do.'

She yawned and laughed. 'I'm not tired.'

'Sleep well. If the storm bothers you, call me. I'm only next door.'

Jessie swallowed painfully. Why did he have to remind her how close he would be? Now her dreams would be haunted by visions of him lying in the Grattons' huge old four-poster bed. He had never liked pyjamas and the thought made her run her tongue nervously over her lips. Why had she agreed to stay? A soaking would have been preferable to putting herself through this torment.

But there was Sam. He was prone to colds. Another soaking might bring on an illness, so there was really no choice.

When Adrian left her alone, she slid out of the robe and under the down quilt. It had a faint tang of moth-balls—which wasn't unpleasant, bringing back memories of visits to her grandmother's house in Adelaide when she was a child.

Thinking of those days, she felt overwhelmingly lonely. Her grandparents were long dead and her father was buried beside them, a victim of a stroke at fifty. Her mother had remarried, and now lived in Queensland. Christmas cards were their only form of communication these days.

Jessie and her mother had never been close. Sometimes Jessie thought her mother envied her the life of a modern woman. If she only knew! Many times, Jessie would gladly have stepped back a generation, to when her only responsibilities were home and hearth.

'You win some, you lose some,' was the way Jo looked at it. Dear Jo. One day she would introduce Adrian to her friend. What would he say when he found out that 'Joe' was a vivacious former ballet dancer with a lot of gypsy in her soul?

Jessie lay awake for a long time, listening to the storm raging outside. She was warm enough under the quilt, but every crash of thunder made her cringe. Only the thought of Adrian, a room away, gave her courage. He would come if she needed him, she had no doubt. But would it stop at offering aid and comfort? It was safer not to find out.

By the time she opened her eyes again, the storm was over and the sun shone out of an impossibly blue sky. Looking out at the gardens, it was hard to believe that the tumult of the previous night had ever happened. Only the stub of burned-out candle, and the battered banks of rhododendrons beneath the window, remained as evidence.

A huge elm had been split almost in two by lightning, its blackened trunk a terrifying testament to the storm's force. Adrian had been right to insist on them staying. They could have been killed by flying debris.

Sam was already up, dressed somewhat haphazardly in his own clothes and watching television, when she came into the kitchen. 'The power must

be back on,' she observed drily. Morning television
was usually forbidden but she decided to be lenient
for once. It was Sunday, and the circumstances were
unusual.

'Have you seen Dr Cole this morning?' she asked
over the blare of the super-heroes theme. How could
anyone with Sam's IQ enjoy such fare?

Guiltily, he looked away at her, then back to the
screen. 'He went out, but he left a letter for you.
It's on the table. And he said I could watch his
television.'

'I'm glad you asked permission,' she said in her
'mother' voice. 'It's just for today, understand?'

His eyes never left the screen. 'Yes, Mum.'

She went to the table, flushing with pleasure as
she beheld the basket of goodies sitting there. It
was the kind delivered by the dial-it services, and
contained every variety of breakfast delicacy from
caviare and strawberries to champagne and orange
juice. She reached for the note tucked under the
handle.

'Sorry I had to leave early,' Adrian wrote. 'I
almost forgot I had a production meeting for the
show. Yes, on a Sunday,' he anticipated the
question which sprang into her mind. 'Enjoy the
breakfast. I'll be back by the time you reach the
coffee stage.'

Disappointment shafted through her. It would
have been much nicer to share the treat with him.
She suppressed the sensation, reminding herself that
he wasn't a part of her life any more. Sam was all
the company she needed.

Still, it wasn't the same sharing caviare on thin
triangles of toast with a six-year-old whose eyes kept

straying to the small screen. His one-word answers hardly passed for conversation.

Resignedly, she gathered the remains of the feast and stacked the dishes in the sink. She was halfway through the washing up when the doorbell rang.

Gorgeous was the only word for the woman to whom she opened the door. Model-slender, she was immaculately groomed, in a beige trouser-suit which screamed designer label. Her face teased Jessie with its familiarity. Where had she seen this woman before?

'Is Dr Cole in?' the caller asked.

That melodious voice! 'You're Davina Davis.' Belatedly, she recognised the television personality. She must be working with Adrian on the new show.

The woman gave a self-conscious smile. 'You guessed it. I'm here for a production meeting with Dr Cole.'

'There's some mistake. He left a note to say he's gone to the meeting.'

Davina Davis sighed prettily. 'The studio can't have told him I planned to meet him here. I'd better wait. He's bound to come back once he realises.'

Taken aback, Jessie showed the woman into Adrian's living-room which was littered with the wine glasses from the night before. The blackout had made tidying up out of the question. She saw Davina's gaze sweep the room then return to her. 'Are you a friend of Dr Cole's?'

'Actually, we're related.' Jessie saw no reason to enlighten her further. She had found a target for her murderous feelings and she didn't like it one bit. She had never been jealous of another woman, but she couldn't fight the feelings which rose in her like a king tide. Was this the real recipient of the breakfast basket?

'Adrian didn't mention he had relatives living with him.'

'I'm not. I live in the gatehouse you passed before you turned into the driveway.'

'Nice place. Pity about the storm damage.'

Jessie's mouth went dry. 'What storm damage?'

'You haven't seen it yet?' Davina sounded genuinely distressed. 'Oh, dear, I don't like to be the bearer of bad news...'

'I'm glad you forewarned me.' Inside, Jessie's heart raced. What had happened to her home? Excusing herself, she went in search of Sam. She would have preferred to inspect the damage without him, but she couldn't leave him with a stranger, and she was desperate to know the worst.

# CHAPTER FIVE

THE gatehouse to the left of the main driveway was half hidden behind azalea bushes. At first, the damage didn't look too bad. The worst didn't become apparent until Jessie pushed open her front gate and approached the old stone lodge.

Sam's hand slid from hers, and she clutched her cheeks in shock. 'Oh, my lord!'

'There's a tree in our living-room.'

Sam was right. The storm had ripped apart the huge elm tree which shaded their front door, spearing a giant branch through the living-room windows. Stained glass littered the cobbled courtyard, and the plush plum-coloured carpet of which she'd been so proud was sodden and strewn with debris.

A linen-covered couch lurched drunkenly across the opening, the Sanderson-print cover making it look like some kind of bizarre plant in the flower-bed. In the midst of the chaos, the weather satellite Sam had been building with his construction set nestled in the fork of the fallen tree like a miniature alien from *The War of the Worlds*.

Sam reached for it, but Jessie held him back. 'Careful, darling, there's broken glass everywhere.'

'I'm glad the tree didn't land on me,' he said cheerfully.

The full horror of it all swept over her, and her knees buckled. If she hadn't grabbed the gatepost, she would have fallen. The tree *could* have landed on Sam. If Adrian hadn't talked them into staying at the main house, her child could have been killed. He loved playing on the floor beside the window.

Tears streamed down her face and she grabbed him in a bear-hug. Alarmed, he tried to squirm free. 'What's the matter, Mum?'

'Nothing, darling. I'm glad the tree didn't land on you. 'Cos I love you more than anything in the world.'

Embarrassed, he did wriggle away. 'Aw, Mum.'

'Don't you "Mum" me. I'm allowed to say I love you if I do.'

'Can I play in the back garden?'

Not so long ago, 'I love you, too,' would have echoed back to her as he hugged her and rained sloppy kisses across her face. At six he was already embarrassed by shows of emotion. His manhood threatened to be a lonely time for her.

She shook off the sentimental feeling. 'You can play in the back garden with your tennis ball, but don't come out here until I tell you it's safe. OK?'

'OK, Mum.' He trotted down the side path, brushing broken branches out of his way. She made a mental note to cut them back as soon as possible.

Her garden was a disaster area. Carefully-tended beds of lobelia and babies' breath, pansies and lavender were flattened by wind and rain.

Her beloved old-fashioned roses, many of them gifts from friends' gardens, spilled over the brick pathway. She tried to right one, then gave up when it toppled sideways on to the litter of petals and buds which now would never burst into bloom.

Heartsick, she picked her way through the debris and unlocked the front door, then laughed at her own foolishness. She could just as easily have stepped through the shattered windows.

The rest of the house looked untouched. A kitchen window was cracked and the french windows in her bedroom had blown open, allowing rain to soak her bed and carpets, but everything else was intact. The radio she switched on—for companionship while she began the clean-up—reported hundreds of houses unroofed by the storm. She should count herself lucky.

Although it was Sunday, the phone book listed several glaziers who operated seven days a week. Three of them told her she would have to join the queue. Tradesmen were at a premium due to the extent of the storm damage.

They advised her to nail some boards across the opening until repairs could be arranged. When would that be? A week or more, judging by the number of calls coming in. Dispiritedly, she hung up.

She was on her knees, gingerly picking fragments of glass out of the carpet, when she heard footsteps on the cobblestones. She looked up to see Joseph Reiner picking his way across the courtyard.

She stood up and brushed wet leaves off her skirt. 'You chose quite a day to come visiting.'

He surveyed the damage with a sympathetic eye. 'It's a shame about your garden. And the house, of course.'

'This room caught the worst of it.' She gestured for him to join her in the ruined living-room. 'Come through to the kitchen. At least it's still in one piece.'

Joseph hesitated. 'I don't want to put you out with all this on your plate.'

'It's all right. I was about to make coffee for myself. It'll be good to have some company.'

He followed her into the kitchen. After the mess of the living-room, it was a pleasant surprise. Apart from a flattened box of herbs on a window ledge and the cracked pane, the room was intact.

Jessie had retained its old-world charm with her choice of dark wood and leadlight doors for the cupboards, marble surfaces and charcoal slate flooring. Despite the damage, it looked cosy and inviting.

Joseph perched on a bar stool on the opposite side of the kitchen bench, and watched while she measured coffee into a filter. 'How are things in the city?'

'Hardly any damage. It seems most of the storm's fury was confined to the hills.'

'I didn't mean the storm. I meant at Grattons. Have you handed in your resignation yet?'

He gave a wry smile. 'Coming so soon after yours, it raised a few eyebrows, but I couldn't stay on under the present management, any more than you could.'

'You'd think the mass exodus would tell them something, wouldn't you?'

He toyed with a salt-shaker in the shape of a duck. 'There are plenty of people willing to work for them on their terms, so they don't care.'

She remembered Sir Mark's comment about Grattons not wanting to lose experienced people.

Evidently it didn't matter to them. The chance of a new contract with fairer terms seemed less likely than ever.

Which reminded her. 'I have good news,' she said, pouring boiling water over the coffee grounds. It hissed and bubbled, then settled down to a steady drip-drip. She got out cream and sugar and put them in front of Joseph.

His sombre expression didn't change. 'I'm glad someone does.'

Pleased to be able to cheer him up, she described her visit to Sir Mark and Lady Gratton. 'So you see, the problem of premises may be solved already,' she finished, on a note of triumph.

Instead of looking pleased, he grew tense. 'You haven't signed anything yet, have you?'

'I wouldn't without consulting you. But I thought you'd be as excited as I am.'

He pushed his hair back with a jerky movement. 'Last week, I would have been.'

'What's happened, Joseph?' She should have realised that something was wrong the moment he arrived, but she had been too preoccupied with her own problems to notice the uncharacteristic slump of his shoulders and the dull look in his eyes. He looked older than when she had last seen him.

'My father died suddenly on Friday night,' he said.

Her hand went to his arm. 'Oh, Joseph, I'm so sorry. Here I am babbling on about business. Your family live in Sydney, don't they?'

He gave a stiff nod. 'They run a paint and wallpaper business in the suburbs. Dad was only sixty-three, that's the worst of it.'

'And your mother? How's she coping?'

'Not at all well. It's the reason I had to see you today, Jessie. I'm flying to Sydney this afternoon.'

She poured coffee into a cup and placed it in front of him. 'Do you have other brothers and sisters?' It was the first time she'd thought to ask him, but their relationship up to now had always been strictly business.

He shook his head and sipped the coffee, wincing as the heat of it met his lips. He added more cream and stirred it thoughtfully. 'I'm an only child. Dad always wanted me to go into the business with him. Reiner and Son,' he said with a far-away look.

She could see the guilt he was labouring under. All the words left unsaid, the gestures unmade, the deeds undone. 'You mustn't torture yourself, Joseph. Your parents must have been pleased that you were happy in the work you chose.'

'They were, I suppose. At least, they never said anything. I'm the one having an attack of the guilts.'

She'd felt the same way when her own father had died, after waiting in vain for a grandchild. It would have made him so happy to know that she was carrying Adrian's child even as he lay in intensive care after his first, massive stroke. But she hadn't even known it herself then.

'You'll feel better when you've seen your mother,' she assured him. 'Going home is the right thing to do.'

He brightened visibly. 'I'm glad you agree, Jessie. I dreaded the thought of telling you.'

Over the rim of her coffee-cup, her eyes narrowed. 'What *are* you trying to tell me, Joseph?'

'I may not come back at all. Mum can't run the family business on her own. She's going to need me.'

A black abyss opened at her feet and she took a step back, recoiling physically from his news. 'But what about our business plans?'

He spread his hands wide. 'You see the position I'm in. My own life is on hold until I see how things are with Mum.'

'But you know I can't start the business alone. And I won't be able to afford an employee at first. If it weren't for Sam...'

'I know, and I hate letting you down. But I don't know what else I can do right now.'

Neither did Jessie, but torturing him with more guilt on her behalf when he was already suffering after the death of his father wasn't going to help. 'It's all right, I'll work something out,' she said, with forced cheerfulness. 'In your shoes, I'd do exactly the same thing.'

'You would? You don't know how much better that makes me feel.'

She shrugged, although she felt like crying inside. 'What else are friends for?'

'Speaking of which...'

Jessie started as Jo Napier came into the room. After years of living together, they seldom bothered to knock at each other's doors. Still, it was a surprise to see her so unexpectedly. 'Where did you spring from?'

'I came in the front way. Your wall was open.'

Jessie set out another cup and saucer but Jo waved them away. 'Not for me, thanks. I heard about the storm damage on the radio and drove up to make sure you and Sam were all right.'

'As you can see, we're shaken but not stirred,' Jessie assured her. 'We spent the night under Adrian's roof.'

Her friend's eyebrows lifted but before she could begin an inquisiton Jessie said quickly, 'You two know each other, don't you?'

Jo nodded cordially, but Jessie wondered how long she would let herself be side-tracked. 'Hello, Joseph. Are you on an errand of mercy, too?'

Quickly, Jessie filled Jo in on Joseph's news, and heard her sharp intake of breath when she mentioned that Joseph might be staying in Sydney. 'But what about...?'

'Not a problem,' Jessie cut in firmly, giving an almost imperceptible shake of her head.

To her credit, Jo got the message at once. 'Of course not. These things have a way of working out.'

Just how they were supposed to work out, Jessie hadn't a clue. Right now, she felt like Scarlett O'Hara, wanting to postpone thinking about any of it until tomorrow. Except that in real life, tomorrow had a way of becoming today. 'Did you bring Nell with you?' she asked.

'She's in the car, fuming with impatience. We're off to visit the dingoes at Cleland Conservation Park and she insisted I ask if Sam can come with us.'

Dingoes were Sam's favourite animals. When one was accused of stealing a camper's baby in a celebrated court case, his sympathies were all with the animals. 'He'd love to, and it would solve a problem for me,' Jessie said.

'I thought so when I saw the mess,' Jo agreed. 'Are you sure I shouldn't stay and help you?'

'You'll be doing me a much bigger favour by looking after Sam.'

'Why don't I keep him overnight and drop him at school in the morning? You can pick him up in the afternoon.'

Impulsively, Jessie hugged her. 'You're an angel of mercy.'

The other woman gave Joseph a wry smile. 'I've been telling her so for years.'

Sam was only too happy to go with Jo and Nell. The prospect of staying overnight appealed even more. He was packed and ready in an amazingly short time, although Jessie had trouble convincing him he would need a few items besides his weather satellite and a book on meteorology which Adrian had given him.

She saw him off, then returned to the kitchen and sank down on a stool opposite Joseph. The day's events were catching up with her and she suddenly felt tired and drained.

'More coffee?' she asked Joseph, as she poured herself a cup.

He glanced at his watch. 'I have to go soon. I feel such a louse, leaving you in the lurch like this.'

She was just about out of reassuring things to say to him. If he stayed much longer, she would start to agree with him. 'Don't torture yourself. What happened isn't your fault. It's nobody's fault.'

He stood up and faced her awkwardly. 'Jessie, you're wonderful.'

Only because she refused to burden him with any more guilt. Inside, she felt like throwing a tantrum even Sam would be ashamed of. Adrian had said she had courage but she hadn't a bottomless pit of it. 'I'll walk you to the door—what's left of it,' she offered. If he didn't leave soon, she *would* break down and cry.

He was silent as she led the way down the hall. In the open doorway, he surprised her by putting his arms around her and kissing her warmly. 'You're a friend in need, Jessie Cole.'

There was a discreet cough a few feet away. She pulled away from Joseph as Adrian strode up the path. Hysterical laughter bubbled in her throat. He was probably going to tell her all about the wonderful Davina Davis, and would be astonished when she threw something at him. There was only so much she could handle in one day.

Joseph regarded the new arrival with interest. 'I thought you moved to the Hills for peace and quiet.'

'Some days it's like Rundle Mall up here,' she said. Since Adrian stood between Joseph and the front gate, she had little choice but to introduce them.

As soon as she mentioned Joseph Reiner's name, Adrian's eyes became shuttered and he ignored the other man's outstretched hand. 'Maybe I should come back later.'

What on earth was the matter with him? Joseph looked nonplussed, but managed to smile. 'There's no need. I'm leaving. I'll send you a postcard to let you know what happens,' he told Jessie.

She gave him a friendly peck on the cheek. 'I hope everything goes well for you.'

He left, but Adrian remained in the doorway, his face as immobile as a statue. 'Is something the matter?' she asked, puzzled.

'I suppose you enjoyed that,' he said coldly.

'Enjoyed what?' He wasn't making any sense... Then it dawned on her. He thought Joseph was the 'Joe' in her life. She had never considered the similarity in her friends' names to be a liability before. It was now.

'Having me catch you in your lover's arms,' he continued in the same icy voice. 'Does it give you a thrill to keep two men on a string?'

'You don't know what you're talking about. And in any case, one of the men cut the string six years ago.'

'I only finished what you started,' Adrian countered angrily.

It was too much. The shock of finding her home in chaos, then discovering that her business plans were also in ruins, began to take its toll. Her limbs trembled and she turned away, but not before he had glimpsed the tell-tale brightness in her eyes.

'Jessica, wait. This wasn't how I meant the conversation to go at all.'

Blinking hard, she brought her head up. 'We do tend to rub each other up the wrong way, don't we?'

He massaged his chin. 'Come to think of it, what else is new?'

She hesitated for the merest moment. 'Would you like to come in for coffee?'

'Actually, I intended to take Sam off your hands for a few hours, if he'd like it.' He surveyed the damaged wall. 'It looks as if you could use the help.'

'His Auntie Drew had the same idea. They've gone to the Cleland Conservation Park and he's staying with her overnight,' she explained, not sure why she felt compelled to add the last bit of information.

'Wise decision.' His tone made it sound as if it was anything but wise, and a strange glint lightened his eyes.

For the first time in over six years, they were truly alone together, Jessie realised. Confusion whirled through her until she forcibly marshalled it. So what if they were alone? It didn't mean anything, couldn't mean anything. She had Sam to consider. And he had Davina Davis.

'I'd like that coffee.' His soft voice startled her out of her reverie.

'Yes, of course, come in. Sorry about the mess.'

'Mess is an understatement,' he echoed. 'You won't fix this lot with a vacuum cleaner.'

Jessie wrinkled her nose. 'I know, I've already tried. But after the storm, every tradesman in Adelaide is booked up for weeks.'

'Perhaps I can help.'

Adrian had never been much of a handyman so the question slipped out before she could stop it. 'How?'

His lop-sided grin did strange things to her insides. 'Fair question. I meant my builders haven't much to do until more bricks are located. I'm paying them a retainer so they may as well work here.'

'I'd have to reimburse you,' she said mechanically.

She saw his eyes darken. 'I hope you'll consider it a favour.'

Mild panic flared inside her. She didn't want favours from Adrian Cole, didn't want to be beholden to him in any way. They were already bound by too many ties. She would be a fool to encourage more. All the same, she heard herself say, 'Thank you. I appreciate the help.'

His mouth twisted into a wry smile. 'Once, you'd have argued and insisted on paying your way.'

'Once, I was a headstrong teenager who didn't know any better,' she had no hesitation in confessing. It was hard to believe she had been only eighteen when they met. It seemed a lifetime ago.

'I was right, you *have* changed,' he stated.

'Not completely,' she felt compelled to warn him.

Adrian gave a heavy sigh. 'You still don't approve of grown men pitting themselves against nature, do you?'

'You make it sound almost respectable.'

Annoyance sparked in his eyes. 'It *is* respectable, damn it! How small the world would be if the early explorers hadn't risked falling off the edge of the world.'

'That was different,' Jessie said stubbornly. 'They had a purpose in their explorations.'

'Modern explorers have their purpose,' he insisted. 'Think how many new products were developed as a result of the space race. Everything from Teflon to Velcro, as well as medical and scientific advances.'

She tossed her head in a defiant gesture. 'Tell that to the widows of the *Challenger* space shuttle crew. Besides, I thought you'd given all that up.'

He frowned. 'It doesn't mean I've changed what I believe in.'

'Neither have I.' It was said so quietly that Jessie wasn't sure Adrian had heard. Only his silence as he followed her into the kitchen told her he had. His presence close behind her was almost tangible. His breath warmed the back of her neck and with each step his hand brushed the small of her back.

She had an instant fantasy of turning around and being welcomed into his arms. It was just as speedily dispelled. Two minutes in each other's company, and already they were arguing as bitterly as ever. Whoever said that opposites attracted couldn't have had them in mind.

Adrian occupied the stool recently vacated by Joseph. His eyes roved around the country kitchen. 'This is cosy. Your own handiwork?'

'Décor by Jessica Cole, accessories by Grattons,' she recited. 'The staff discount helped a lot.'

'The last few years haven't been easy for you, have they?'

His sympathy was the last thing Jessie wanted. 'I've coped,' she said, with a shrug of her shoulders.

'And coped well. This house, your son—you should be proud.'

The way he said 'your son' made her feel anything but proud. She felt ashamed of keeping the truth from him. He had as much right to be proud of Sam as she had. If only she believed he had changed enough to be content with sharing their child. But he'd said his beliefs remained the same. She couldn't take the risk.

She decided to inject a healthy dose of reality into the conversation. 'Thanks for providing

breakfast this morning. I hope Miss Davis didn't
mind too much.'

A puzzled frown creased his brow. 'Why should
she? Once we sorted out the mix-up over the
meeting, it was a simple matter of rescheduling it.
No harm done.'

Not unless you counted the harm to her pride,
knowing that his elaborate breakfast preparations
were probably intended for someone else. Perhaps
the basket wasn't even his doing—it was the sort
of thing television people did all the time. It wasn't
any concern of hers in any case... Except for a
feeling of betrayal which refused to go away.

The coffee was still bubbling. As she poured
some, she was keenly aware of Adrian watching her
every move. The intensity of his scrutiny unnerved
her and she sloshed coffee into his saucer. When
she reached for it, he forestalled her. 'Don't fuss.
It's fine as it is.'

She sat down opposite him. 'It was good of you
to think of entertaining Sam.'

'I had hoped to spend the day with you both.
But I understand now why you didn't want to wait.'

He thought she had hurried home to meet
Joseph. 'I was worried about the house,' she said
with complete accuracy.

He rested his forearms on the counter-top, the
masculine hairs on the backs of them glinting in
the sunlight which spilled between them through
the cracked window pane. 'Your goodbye to your
friend sounded somewhat final.'

Why wouldn't he be side-tracked? 'It was,' she
said, settling for the literal truth. 'Joseph's father

died suddenly and he's going back to Sydney to take over the family business.'

Something unfathomable gleamed in Adrian's gaze as he looked at her. 'You don't sound unduly upset about it.'

'I'm not, except...' She had almost confessed about the business she and Joseph were supposed to be starting. Adrian didn't know she was unemployed yet.

His eyebrow angled curiously. 'Except?'

What was the use? He would find out as soon as he spoke to Mark and Susan. 'Joseph and I were to be partners in a decorating business,' she admitted, unable to keep a bleak note out of her voice.

'And now he's left town.' Did she imagine it or was there satisfaction in the statement? 'What will you do now?'

'I don't know. My contract at Grattons is finished. I hope I can find a similar job elsewhere.'

'Not many of those around,' Adrian mused. 'The days of the small family firm are almost over. Still, I may be able to help until you find what you want.'

Defiance flashed in her eyes. 'I can manage, thanks.'

He understood the reason for her objection at once. 'I wasn't offering money. I need your help, Jessica.'

It was the last thing she'd expected him to say. Adrian had never admitted to needing her for anything. She was the stay-at-home wife, ready to welcome the weary traveller back from the wars. He had never once asked her to go with him. 'This is sudden, isn't it?' she asked.

'Not at all. I meant to discuss it with you when I got back from the meeting, but you'd already left. I need your help with Gratton Park.'

'From what I've seen, you have an army of assistants swarming all over the place.'

'But none with your interest, or your skill, to pull the project together.'

Her eyes narrowed with suspicion. 'How do you know I'd be interested?'

'The way you talked about the history of the place. You've already done the homework. All you have to do is bring it to life as it was in its heyday.'

'It would be a challenge and it wouldn't be cheap.' Almost against her will, the idea shaped itself in Jessie's brain. There was so much she could do with a place the size of Gratton Park. She knew Adrian's tastes and the history of the house. The possibilities tantalised her.

'Money isn't a problem,' he assured her. 'I lived cheaply in the jungle, and my investments happily multiplied while I was away, so you can indulge yourself, your own fee included.'

She would be working for Adrian. The reality hit her like a shower of icy water. Overseeing the decoration of someone's home meant working closely with them day by day. Did she really want to see so much of Adrian? And what about the risk that he would find out the truth about Sam?

'Will you do it?' he pressed.

'I need time to think. It's a wonderful offer, but...'

'But I'm not Joe,' he said with such savagery that she looked at him in astonishment.

'This has nothing to do with him.' It had everything to do with her feelings for Adrian himself, which had been reawakened the moment she saw him again. If she was to have any peace of mind at all, she needed to deal with her feelings and get him out of her system. And she couldn't do it by running away from him.

Still, she balked at a final commitment. 'I'll take a look at the job,' she promised. 'Even if I don't take it on, I can advise you on what needs to be done.'

He drained his coffee-cup and stood up. 'In that case, we may as well get started. Agreed?'

'Well, yes ... but ...'

The rest of her demur was drowned out by the roaring sound of stone tearing from stone and the crash of glass and timber. As a grey cloud enveloped them, Adrian pulled her against him. Choking on dust, she buried her head against the reassuring wall of his chest, feeling the strength of his arms enfolding her. His voice vibrated in her ear. 'What the hell was that?'

## CHAPTER SIX

HOLDING tightly on to Adrian's hand, Jessie surveyed the damage in horrified fascination. 'The whole front wall's gone,' she whispered, shock almost robbing her of her voice.

'The storm damage must have been worse than it appeared.' His fingers tightened their grip on her hand. 'When I think of you standing under that thing!' Horror rang in his voice.

Dust rose from the rubble in a silver cloud. 'I guess it wasn't my turn,' she said shakily. 'What am I going to do now?'

'One thing is certain, you can't stay here.' Before she could protest, Adrian offered the one argument she couldn't refute. 'It isn't safe for Sam until you have the place professionally inspected and the damage repaired.'

'You're right. I'll check into a hotel tonight and look for other accommodation in the morning.'

'Whatever for? There's plenty of room at Gratton Park.'

Shock must be fuddling her brain. 'You mean move in with you?'

Adrian's hard gaze transfixed her. 'Not in the literal sense. But you and Sam are welcome to use my spare rooms. It would save you having to disrupt Sam's schooling.'

Jessie had wanted to prove to herself that she was over Adrian and this was more of a trial by fire than she'd bargained for. But it was hard to deny his reasoning. 'All right,' she agreed. Then it hit her. Sam was away until tomorrow.

'Maybe I should stay here until Sam comes home,' she suggested.

Anger blazed in his hazel eyes, shooting the irises with golden threads. 'Are you crazy? The house isn't safe. Who knows what other hidden damage the storm may have done.'

Startled by his vehemence, she gave in without further argument, packing some things for herself and Sam while Adrian stood guard.

The speed with which events were moving left her feeling breathless. Only moments ago, the idea of working for Adrian had alarmed her. Now she was actually moving in with him. Into his house, she corrected herself mentally. The difference hardly seemed to matter at this point.

'Is that everything?' Adrian demanded.

Travelling frequently on business had made her into an efficient packer. She fastened the case with a decisive snap. 'It will do. I can come back for anything else I need.'

'Then for goodness' sake, let's get out of here.'

Alarmed by his impatience, she hesitated. 'I must be putting you out.'

His long fingers clamped over her wrist. 'We'll discuss it later. Come on.'

Choking back her anger, Jessie allowed him to pull her out of the room, her case hefted easily in his free hand. Catching sight of them in a hall mirror, she thought they looked like two teenagers running away from home. The image vaporised the last of her annoyance. Typically, Adrian was doing what he thought best regardless of other people's sensitivities. The building was unsafe, therefore they should get out as efficiently as possible. To him, her reluctance to leave was illogical.

He deposited her outside the front door. 'I'll get Sam's case.'

Moments later he was back with the small suitcase she'd packed with her son's clothes, books and essential toys. Not that Sam possessed many toys. He preferred to make his own from construction sets and odds and ends. But he was attached to a blue rabbit, high IQ or not.

'Thank goodness, you brought Hindsight,' she said, noticing the stuffed animal under Adrian's arm.

He looked at it, then cocked a quizzical eyebrow at her. 'Hindsight?'

She sighed. 'I know. I tried for Fluffy, but Sam insisted on his choice of name. All because he heard me say that, with hindsight, rabbits would never have been introduced into Australia.'

Adrian held the rabbit up by its pink satin-lined ears. 'So this is the cause of all that soil erosion. I often wondered.'

For once, the silence was companionable as they picked their way across the debris of her front garden, and turned in to the driveway to Gratton Park.

'I'll send someone over to board your place up,' Adrian said when they were safely inside.

'While you arrange it, I'll phone Sam's Auntie Drew and tell her what's happened,' she volunteered. 'She has an answering machine——' she anticipated his question.

She was laughing when she finished recording her message, and then had to explain that Jo's machine was answered by a Sylvester Stallone imitator. 'He threatens to send Rambo around to punch out the lights of anyone who doesn't leave a message after the tone sounds.'

He smiled. 'No wonder Sam's devoted to her. She sounds like quite a lady. I must meet her some time.'

Alarm bells sounded in her head. If she introduced them, she could hardly expect him to call Jo 'Auntie Drew', and there would go her precious cover story. She murmured something non-committal.

The breakfast basket, greatly depleted, was still on the kitchen table, and Adrian fished the champagne bottle out of it. 'Like some?'

It was altogether too tempting. Already, there was a feeling of familiarity about the scene, as if they'd played it hundreds of times before. They had, in a way, before his obsession with danger had driven them apart. 'I'd rather discuss the house,' she dissembled.

Annoyance flickered across his face before he managed a smile and replaced the bottle. 'Suit yourself. But wouldn't you rather get settled in first?'

'I suppose so. Shall I have the same room I had last night?'

'I thought it was a bit small for a longer stay, so I put your case in my room.'

Nerve-stretching seconds passed while she fought the tumult of sensations his statement induced. A reckless urge to agree rioted through her until she quelled it. 'The single room will be fine.'

'Too late. I've already moved my stuff in there.' He caught the wild look in her eyes. 'Did you think . . . you *did* think I meant us to share it!' The heat flooding her cheeks confirmed his suspicion. 'Jessica, I know how you feel about me now. I don't intend to take advantage of this situation.' He clenched and unclenched his fingers in a gesture which bespoke his frustration with her. 'Living in the jungle hasn't made me totally uncivilised.'

Jessie was ashamed of her suspicions, and even more annoyed with her body for reacting to them almost independently of her common sense. 'I know,' she whispered. 'I'm sorry.'

He accepted her apology with a tight nod of his head, then led the way to the master bedroom suite which she'd visited once or twice before when Susan was ill in bed.

She was pleased to find the bedroom untouched. Unlike the rest of the house, which owed allegiance to no particular period, this room was definitely Italianate—a legacy of a Renaissance promotion Sir Mark had undertaken at Grattons.

A self-confessed Naples enthusiast, he had picked the eyes out of the furniture collection imported for the promotion. Most of it had found its way into this suite.

A gloriously ornate carved bedhead drew her eye to a massive, old-fashioned bedstead covered in a tapestry spread. The wardrobes were delicately patterned with insets of olive green which Susan had repeated on the walls and ceilings. Whimsical pieces of statuary dotted the room.

'I'm glad you haven't changed this room,' she told Adrian.

'I don't plan to, unless you recommend it. I mean you to have a free hand.'

She surveyed the room with shining eyes. 'But not here. I couldn't possibly improve on this.'

His nod signalled his approval. He rested a hand on the head of a gilded 'blackmoor'. 'It reminds me of a stage set, out of *The Merchant of Venice*, say.'

'Or *Romeo and Juliet*.'

' "My only love sprung from my only hate, Too early seen unknown, and known too late." '

The soft quotation made Jessie catch her breath, but when she looked up, Adrian had turned away. 'I'll leave you to unpack, then we can talk about the house.'

He was standing amid the debris of the dining-room when she joined him. The antique table and chairs were hidden under dust covers and the worn Axminster carpeting had been rolled up, revealing dusty tallow-wood floorboards which just might polish to a glorious patina.

He caught her eyeing the floorboards. 'My thoughts exactly.'

It was impossible not to laugh. 'How do you know what I'm thinking?'

'You never could hide your feelings from me, Jessica.'

Her wide-eyed gaze met his in shocked surprise. She had forgotten, or had made herself forget, how well he could read her responses. Coming here was a mistake. How long would it be before he guessed that there was no other man in her life, because none of them held a candle to Adrian himself? Once he knew that, the next step—working out the identity of Sam's father—would be easy.

He came closer. 'For instance, right now you're wondering if you were right to come here. I told you, there's nothing to worry about.'

His hand grazed the side of Jessie's face, and she drew a rasping breath. 'Is this what you call nothing?'

'You didn't always flinch from my touch,' he reminded her huskily.

'It was different then,' she defended herself.

'Is it so different now?' His hand slid down her breast and rested on her heart, reading its frantic beating through his fingers. She was torn between wanting to push him away, and wanting to gather his hand in hers and crush his fingertips to her lips.

Both his hands were clasped in hers before she realised she had moved. 'Oh, Adrian.' The words came out on a wistful sigh.

'You still have skin like satin and hair like silk,' he said, his fingers tightening in hers. His lips found their way to the crown of her head. As he kissed it, liquid fire raced along her veins and her pulses hammered a warning tattoo.

His hold was light. She could spin out of reach any time she wanted to. Yet she stayed where she was, quivering like a butterfly on a new leaf, her senses beating the air like wings, yet refusing to help her take flight.

'Jessica.' He made her name sound like a benediction. His fingers threaded through her hair, easing her head back so she stared wildly at him, her lips gently parted as she waited for his kiss.

The delay was exquisite. His breath fanned her face, his mouth inches away, yet resisting her obvious invitation. His eyes mesmerised her, their smoky depths afire with golden lights which played over her like flames.

The heat from his touch seared her very soul as he caressed her with practised ease. He knew exactly where to touch her to arouse her to fever pitch, how to pleasure her with each feathery stroke of his fingers. Crushed against him, her breasts felt sensitised almost beyond endurance. How could she have forgotten the heaven of being in his arms?

In truth, she hadn't forgotten, not one minuscule sensation. They were filed away in the recesses of her soul, awaiting the kiss which would awaken her from her Sleeping Beauty trance.

'How could I have stayed away so long?' he murmured, his voice muffled by the pressure of his lips against the creamy expanse of her throat.

An arctic wind swept through her mind, chilling the fires which had threatened to consume her. What was she doing, letting him have such an effect on her? He *had* stayed away for all those long, lonely years. There was every chance he would do so again. Letting herself feel this way was insane. Hadn't she learned *anything* in the last six years?

Her tension transmitted itself to Adrian and he regarded her with a puzzled expression. 'You do want me, don't you, Jessica?'

'I can hardly deny it, can I?' The strength of her response had been in every breath she took.

'Then what is it?'

Her hands fluttered in the air. 'You ... This ... What we were doing... It's all wrong!'

'For me, it felt right.' He paced to the china-cabinet, thrust aside its dust cover, and took out a whisky decanter and glasses. His hands were less than steady as he poured.

Jessie shook her head when he offered a drink to her. With a 'suit yourself' shrug, he set it down and sipped his own. 'I don't get it. You say it's over between you and Joe, yet you won't give me a chance. Is it because of what I said about Sam?'

'You did accuse me of cheating on you,' she reminded him carefully.

'Things were going wrong for us and I accept some of the responsibility. If you hadn't thought our marriage was already over, you wouldn't have looked at another man.'

Did he have to be so reasonable? It was almost easier to take when he thought she had had a child by her lover. His generosity shamed her for keeping the truth from him. She bowed her head as tears trickled under tightly closed lashes.

He cupped her chin and drew her head up, meeting her bright gaze with gentle frankness. 'I won't say I'm happy about it, Jessica. No man worthy of the name could be. But you must have been desperately unhappy to look elsewhere for fulfilment.'

That much, at least, was true, and she nodded miserably. 'I was.'

'Then maybe it isn't too late for us. Since I won't be climbing mountains or trekking across polar ice any more, maybe we'll have a chance to work it out.'

A hope so sweet that it was almost painful swelled inside Jessie, and she swallowed convulsively. He was saying the one thing she longed to hear above all else, the one thing which could give them a chance. Dared she trust him?

'I know it will take time,' he said, sensing her doubts. 'Take all you need. Work on the house, no strings attached. I won't pressure you into anything you aren't ready for. All right?'

'All right.' Jessie's throat was so choked with emotion that the words were barely audible. But Adrian heard her and nodded, then pushed the whisky towards her. This time she accepted it, and silently drank a toast to 'hope'.

Even after a week, it was still a shock to wake up and find herself at Gratton Park, living on the other side of what Jo had dubbed 'Adrian's Wall'. True to his word, Adrian hadn't pressured Jessie into intimacy, and they had worked side by side on the house whenever he could spare the time from his book and television show.

Already they had made great strides on the library and formal dining-rooms. Both were now panelled in cedar, looking as they would have done a hundred years before. The floors looked as good as she'd hoped, polishing to a brilliant gloss which set off Adrian's handmade rugs, collected on his travels.

'Susan will love to see the place looking so splendid,' she told him, when they finally removed the covers from the antique dining furniture.

The walls had been papered in a silvery grey with a small plum-coloured motif, echoed in the heavy curtains and padded pelmets. The chairs had been re-upholstered in the same silver-grey, and the effect was stunning.

'She always said she wanted to restore the house,' Adrian agreed. 'But there was always another charity or committee to keep her from getting around to it.'

'Worthy as her causes are, I think the real reason was because she didn't want to part with her clutter,' Jessie confided. 'Their new place looks just like this one did before it was touched.'

Susan was the first to agree with her when Jessie made good her promise to take Sam to visit them. He looked on Sir Mark as a surrogate grandfather, and was bursting to see them again.

'I've got so much news,' he said importantly. Sir Mark listened gravely as the six-year-old described his visit to the dingoes a week before, and the workings of the toy satellite he had finished building with Adrian's help.

Susan's eyes twinkled at Jessie over the top of Sam's head. 'It sounds as if Auntie Drew has a rival for your son's affections.'

'I'm afraid so.' A pang shot through Jessie. It was true that Sam was becoming increasingly attached to Adrian. The feeling was mutual, judging by the amount of time Adrian found in his crowded schedule to spend with the child. He was now determined to be a meteorologist like Dr Cole when he grew up.

'Have you seen much of Adrian since he got back?' she asked Susan.

'He came to the city to do some research for his book, and dropped in for coffee,' she said. 'He's looking well. Could it have anything to do with your moving into the main house?'

Jessie felt the colour seep into her cheeks. 'I haven't moved in, as you put it. I'm staying there until the storm damage to the gatehouse is repaired.'

Susan gave her a knowing look, but didn't pursue the subject. 'How does Sam like his new surroundings?' she asked.

Sam loved being anywhere that Adrian was, but Jessie felt it was wiser not to say so. 'He loves having the grounds to play in,' she replied instead.

An anxious frown creased Susan's face. 'You won't let him go near the creek, will you?'

'He knows he has to stay in sight of the house,' Jessie reassured the older woman. Some of the local children did play near the creek, attracted by the rock formations which arose on each side of it. It was a perfect place for the imagination to run riot, adapting itself to the surface of an alien planet or the wild west, as a child's fancy chose. But it was no place for a six-year-old.

Susan patted her hand. 'I don't know why I worry. You're a model mother, dear.'

Sam's head came up. 'She doesn't go to work any more, either.'

Jessie gave a startled smile. 'Is that a good thing or a bad thing, sweetheart?'

'A good thing,' he said decisively. 'It means you're a real mother.'

'But I was always a real mother,' she protested, feeling a twinge of anxiety. Sam had never objected to her working, as far as she knew.

'No, you weren't. Before, you didn't make me milk and biscuits when I came home from school.'

'But Auntie Drew did, didn't she?'

'Yes, but she's Nell's mother.'

He made it all sound so clear-cut. She had never dreamed that Sam resented her frequent absences on business.

Susan sensed her despair. 'Don't take it too seriously, dear. Before long, he'll be complaining that you're around too much and interfering in his life.'

'I suppose you're right.' Still, finding that Sam felt neglected settled on her like a weight. She was glad when it was time for them to leave.

'Dr Cole is taking us to the television studio this afternoon,' Sam announced, as they were leaving.

Sir Mark looked impressed. 'Are you going to be a TV star?'

Disgust tugged at Sam's mouth. 'Of course not. Only super-heroes go on TV. We're going to watch Dr Cole make his programme.'

Susan smiled teasingly. 'Does that make Dr Cole a super-hero, then?'

Unaware that he was being teased, Sam looked thoughtful. 'I don't know. He doesn't fly or anything, but he does amazing things.'

You can say that again, Jessie told herself as they drove off. Adrian Cole, super-hero. Whatever next?

Adrian had left their names at the reception desk when they arrived at the television studio. Over the building, a giant transmitter tower sparkled in the afternoon sunshine. Sam's eyes held a matching sparkle as he took in the wonders around them. 'Will we see any super-heroes?' he asked.

His enthusiasm was infectious. Even when Adrian was a TV weatherman, she had never visited the studio, and she was as starry-eyed as Sam. 'You never know what we'll see,' she compromised.

They were escorted through a maze of corridors, behind sheets of scenery as tall as buildings. Thick black cables snaked everywhere underfoot. 'Here's the *Edge of Reality* set,' announced the young woman who had fetched them from reception.

'It's fantastic,' Sam breathed, awed by the bright lights and glittering set confronting them. It was designed to look like the view from a mountain peak, the endless vista stretching behind two presenters' chairs, and framed by a window which was empty of glass.

Jessie touched two fingers to her lips. 'Sssh, honey.'

'It's all right, they aren't recording yet,' the assistant told her. 'You'll be warned when to be quiet.'

She ushered them to the front of a bank of seats which reminded Jessie of a university lecture-theatre. There was no studio audience for *Edge of Reality*, so the seats were empty. They sat down in the darkness, dazzled by the bright lights in front of them.

Sam's eyes swivelled everywhere, but Jessie's were drawn to the tall figure in the centre of the set. The lights gave him an aura of power and authority, and her heart swelled as she watched him. His suit had been specially tailored for the programme and skimmed his athletic proportions, accentuating the breadth of his shoulders and the narrowness of his hips and long, muscular legs.

While he discussed something with a technician, she could look her fill at him for the first time since he got back.

It was a slightly unreal feeling. All those years she had believed he was lost to her. Now he was back, and there was a chance that things could be all right for them. It was more than she had dreamed of. So much more that her chest tightened as she considered how she would feel if it came to nothing.

Adrian saw her and gestured for her to join him. 'Sit here and mind Mummy's handbag,' she told Sam. He swelled with importance and clutched the bag tightly. 'I'll be right back.'

Shielding her eyes from the bright lights, she picked her way across the sea of cables. Adrian took her arm and guided her to the centre of the set. 'Jessica Cole, this is Tom Holland, our producer,' he introduced her. At the mention of her name, the producer's eyebrows lifted, but he made no comment. From what she'd read about show-business relationships, their situation wasn't even unusual.

'Welcome to the madhouse!' Tom Holland said, shaking her hand.

'What's happening now?' she asked.

The producer rolled his eyes. 'We're waiting for a satellite link-up with an Alaskan dog-sled race,' he told her. 'Adrian's interviewing some of the contestants for tonight's episode.'

'It sounds exciting.'

'Bit of a change for you, eh, Adrian?' one of the camera operators quipped.

Adrian gave him a good-natured grin. 'Why should it be?'

'Sitting here in a cosy studio, watching other people risk their necks,' the man went on. 'I thought you'd be like one of the huskies, straining to get out there.'

Adrian laughed, but his jaw tightened and a pulse jumped in his throat. Alarm flared inside Jessie, but she resisted it. 'This is still an important link, surely?' she asked, hearing the false note in her voice.

'I think I can handle this, thanks,' Adrian replied, his voice fairly vibrant with resentment. What had she done except reassure him that his role was as vital as ever? Or didn't he think so? Was this all an act to assuage her fears? Her hand went to her throat in an involuntary gesture of fear.

The producer listened to something on his headphones, and made a thumbs-up gesture to some figures she could see in a lighted room high above the studio. 'Satellite connection in five minutes,' he informed the floor crew.

Adrian's expression was still cold when she touched his arm and murmured her good wishes. 'Shall we wait for you when this is over?' she asked.

'It's best if you don't. Recording could take hours and there's a production meeting straight afterwards.'

'I see.' Jessie felt very alone as she made her way back to Sam, to watch the taping of the segment. Sam was talking happily to someone, and she tensed when she saw who it was. 'Hello, Miss Davis.'

'Davina, please.' The woman's smile was dazzling but completely genuine.

Jessie felt ashamed of her instinctive reaction, and smiled back. 'Thanks for keeping Sam company.'

'No trouble at all. I was explaining some of the studio procedure to him. How old is he? Eight or nine?'

'Six,' Jessie said, pride creeping in despite herself. She saw Davina's amazement. 'He's advanced for his age.'

'You can say that again.' She hugged Sam, who looked put out by the presumption. 'He acts as if he understands everything I told him.'

He gave her a look of utter disgust. 'I did. But you're wrong about those people in that room up there. They aren't angels. It's called a master control room and they tell the people down here what to do. Dr Cole told me.'

Davina accepted the rebuke good-naturedly, and Jessie found herself warming to her even more. 'Goodbye, *Sesame Street*, hello *Quantum*,' Davina said ruefully. 'I won't try to patronise you again, I promise.'

But Sam's attention had already shifted to the set, where Adrian was running through some lines. The insulated floor and walls soaked up the sound so they could hardly hear what he was saying.

'Are you involved in this?' Jessie asked Davina Davis.

There was a shower of tawny hair as the woman shook her head. 'No, this is between Adrian and the satellite hook-up. His subject will appear on that screen over there. The monitor,' she added, for Sam's benefit. 'Mine is the next segment.'

'You put in long hours,' Jessie said with sympathy.

'We sure do. I was in the studio at five this morning for the AM Show.' Davina pulled a face, then brightened. 'But I'm determined to last through to the party tonight.'

Party was Sam's favourite word after dingo and he regarded her with renewed interest. 'Is it someone's birthday?'

'As a matter of fact, it is. The producer's. Are you staying?'

Adrian had made it clear that he didn't want Jessie there, and now she saw why. He would be otherwise engaged. For a moment she wondered if she'd done the right thing in refusing his advances when she moved in to Gratton Park. Had she driven him into Davina's company? In Adrian's eyes, she could hardly complain if so. After all, as far as he knew, she had Joe.

# CHAPTER SEVEN

TEN. Eleven. Twelve. One.

The grandfather clock counted out the hours with agonising precision. Why couldn't she go to sleep? Jessie pummelled her pillow into yet another shape and buried her head in it, but oblivion refused to come. She told herself it was sheer stupidity, but she couldn't stop herself counting the hours until she heard Adrian's firm tread on the stairs.

Was it her imagination, or did his steps hesitate outside her door? She slowed her breathing and lay still, but he didn't look in. Moments later, she heard his door open and close again.

There was no sign of him when she came down to breakfast next morning, but he'd left a note saying he had an early call at the television studio and would see her later. Why had he bothered coming home at all?

'Why are you angry, Mum?' Sam asked her, as she prepared breakfast.

'I'm not angry!' She slammed another pot down hard on the stove. It was a good question. Why should she care if Adrian stayed out till all hours partying with Davina Davis? It was really none of her business.

'Mum, tell me again about my daddy.'

Jessie's spirits plummeted. Why now, of all times? While Adrian was missing, she could talk about him in the past tense. Now she couldn't do it without lying to her son. 'What do you think he was like?' she asked.

He stirred his cereal thoughtfully. 'I think he was like Dr Cole,' he decided. 'I think he was real smart and had adventures all over the world.'

The ground slid away from under her feet. Her mouth felt dry. Could Sam possibly sense the link between himself and Adrian? If he could, what did Adrian think? Her blank mind registered the sound of a car horn outside. 'There's your friend, Daniel, come to pick you up for school,' she said, blessing the diversion.

He regarded her scornfully. 'It's Daniel's mother. Daniel can't drive.' Then his look turned anxious. 'You won't forget our picnic this afternoon, will you?'

She made the time-honoured gesture. 'Cross my heart. I'll have everything ready by the time you get home. Now scoot.'

Moments later, Sam was strapped into the back seat beside his school friend, their heads almost touching as they exchanged news. It was left to Daniel's mother to wave goodbye.

Feeling wrung out, Jessie came inside and made herself a cup of coffee. The closeness of this morning's call made it obvious that she'd have to decide what to tell Sam about his father—and soon. The questions would only become more pressing. He never abandoned a line of enquiry once it caught his imagination.

'Relax, it could be ages before he raises it again,' Jo reassured her, when she telephoned her friend in despair.

'We should never have moved into this house,' Jessie said.

'What else could you do? Your own isn't habitable yet, is it?'

'The builder found cracks in the foundations so it could be another week or more before we can move back in. Oh, Jo, it's all so complicated. I live in dread that Sam will forget and call you by your name. He's always talking about you and Nell.'

There was a long pause. 'Maybe it's time you told Adrian the truth.'

Fear clutched at Jessie's heart and she shook her head furiously, then realised that Jo couldn't see the gesture. 'You know why I can't. It's too big a risk.'

'Adrian might be more reasonable than you think. You said yourself that he's changed since he went away.'

'He's more settled. I don't know, Jo. I wish there was a way to be sure.'

'There is—it's called trust,' Jo said gently. 'To change the subject, has Sir Mark had any luck convincing Grattons to improve your contract?'

'Not a chance. I took Sam to visit them yesterday and Mark was full of apologies. He said everyone's being offered the same deal, take it or leave it.'

'Then you were right to leave it,' Jo assured her. 'Don't worry, something will turn up soon. In the meantime, I hear you're doing wonders with Gratton Park.'

Jessie twisted the telephone cord between her fingers. 'You must come and see it soon.'

Her friend's hollow laugh rang down the line. 'When Adrian isn't around—I know.' Jessie heard voices in the background, then Jo came back on the line. 'I must go. I've got a class in ten minutes.'

'We *will* get together soon,' Jessie vowed. She owed her friend too much to let this cloak-and-dagger existence come between them.

Later, as she packed a basket for the picnic she had promised Sam, she reached another conclusion. She would have to move out of Gratton Park, even if it meant finding other accommodation until her house was safe to occupy.

Unaccountably, the idea filled her with despair.

A picnic with Sam was just the antidote she needed. As usual when he returned from school, he was bursting with pent-up energy and ran on ahead as they made their way behind the house, to where the land fell away to a heavily wooded gorge, ending in a creek-bed some thirty metres below.

'Wait for me at the rim of the gorge, won't you?' she called as he raced off.

'OK. Bet I'm first to see a wombat,' he yelled back.

She had already spotted one of the lumbering marsupials, but didn't spoil his fun. 'Let's try for a koala today,' she suggested, and he switched his attention to the eucalypts which towered above them.

Gratton Park was paradise for a child, she thought, as she followed Sam more slowly, carrying the picnic basket. If they left here, they would miss the freedom of the valley, with its abundant plant and animal life. It was sometimes hard to believe

they were only a few miles from the city of
Adelaide.

The Adelaide Hills were built on a spine of rock
thrust up from sea-level in prehistoric times. Part
of the land had sunk, creating Spencer Gulf and
the salt-lake basins further inland. The other part
had risen, creating gorges and deep ravines where
creeks bubbled and waterfalls spilled among Eden-
like forests of eucalypts and native vegetation. Rock
climbers and bushwalkers came from all over
Australia to explore these hills, while she and Sam
enjoyed them as a back garden.

'Come on, Mum,' Sam called impatiently, when
her reverie delayed her too long. He hopped from
one foot to the other near the rim of the gorge.

She spread their rug on a rocky outcrop and set
out cold chicken, crusty bread, cheese and fruit.
Wombats were forgotten as Sam launched himself
at the food.

Ten minutes later, she was startled to hear a familiar voice. 'Hello, mind if we join you?'

Around a mouthful of chicken, Sam said, 'Mum,
it's Dr Cole and that lady.'

'Miss Davis, and don't talk with your mouth full,'
she said automatically. The sun had just gone in
on her day. Evidently most of last night and this
morning weren't enough for Adrian. He had to
bring Davina home with him as well.

Her smile was strained. 'Hello. You're welcome,
of course, but I doubt if there's enough for four.'

A rucksack dangled from Adrian's hand. 'When
I saw the two of you heading this way, I brought
extra.'

She made room for them on the rug and Davina
gave a sigh of contentment as she lifted her face to
the sun. She looked more beautiful than ever in an
off-the-shoulder floral sundress and matching
enamel hoop earrings. Alongside her, Jessie felt
scruffy in her jeans and hand-printed T-shirt.

'This is bliss after being cooped up in the studio
for days,' Davina said.

Adrian reached into his bag and pulled out more
bread and cheese and a bottle of Chablis from a
local winery. Condensation sparkled on the glass
like dew. Three acrylic wine glasses appeared next.
He'd thought of everything. 'I hope you don't mind
us interrupting your picnic?' he asked.

Why couldn't Adrian have come alone? Sharing
the splendid afternoon would have been per-
fection, then. As it was, she felt like the proverbial
fifth wheel. The only one who didn't seem to mind
was Sam, who looked thrilled to see his new mentor.

'Course we don't mind, do we, Mum?' he said
heartily. 'You can teach me some more cloud
formations.'

Davina pulled a face. 'Sounds like a fun afternoon.' She looked at Jessie. 'Are they always like
this?'

The other woman's warmth made Jessie smile
back. 'Usually. The other day, they spent an hour
discussing highs, lows and fronts.'

'Whatever happened to *Play School*?' Davina
asked, rolling her eyes.

'It lasted until he was two.' Then it came back
to her. 'You used to be one of the presenters, didn't
you?'

'For my sins.' Davina held her hands up at shoulder height, palms pointed down, and trilled, '"I'm a little teapot, short and stout."'

Jessie couldn't imagine Davina as short and stout, but she laughed at the picture she presented. 'I loved that song. I was devastated when Sam graduated to watching *Beyond 2000*.'

'I can believe it. Adrian told me what a bright lad he is. At the party last night...'

Jessie was aware that they now had Adrian's undivided attention. 'What are you two gossiping about?' he asked, sitting up.

An icy sensation drifted over Jessie. It was obvious that he hadn't meant Davina to mention the party which had kept them out until one this morning. 'I understood it was a meeting,' she said, with deceptive calm. Inside, she was seething. What Adrian did might not concern her, but there was no need to lie about it.

Davina's smile widened. 'It was held in the boardroom at the studio, but there the similarity ended, wouldn't you say, Adrian?'

'I'm sure Jessie isn't interested in the crew's antics,' he demurred. 'Would you like some more chicken?'

The other woman stretched languidly and stood up. 'No thanks, I'm full. I'm going to walk some of it off. I shan't be long.' With graceful movements, she walked away.

An uncomfortable silence settled between them. Sam was exploring an ants' nest with a twig and had his back to them. Davina was out of earshot. Adrian had the grace to look discomfited. 'I suppose you're wondering why I didn't mention the party before you left last night?'

Jessie toyed with her wine glass. 'It's nothing to do with me.'

'But you *are* annoyed, and you have a right to be.'

'Only because you felt the need to lie to me,' Jessie said. It was the only justification for her feeling of betrayal.

Adrian twisted a blade of grass between his fingers. 'As a matter of fact, it wasn't a lie as far as I knew. When I said we had a production meeting after the show, I thought I was telling the truth.'

Her puzzled glance went to his face. 'I don't understand.'

'It was a surprise party for our producer, Tom Holland.' She nodded, remembering the introduction. 'We worked together most of the day so the others couldn't tell me about their plan without tipping him off.'

Elation surged through her until she throttled it back. 'You don't owe me any explanations,' she insisted.

For some reason, this intensified his look of irritation. 'Then you don't care about not being invited?'

Thinking of the long, sleepless hours waiting for him to come home, she felt foolish. Where was her precious plan to prove she was over him now? 'I couldn't care less about the party,' she said with absolute candour.

Being left out of a social engagement wasn't the problem. It was the thought of him spending those hours with Davina Davis. Which proved how far she still had to go to cut her emotional ties to him.

Adrian stood up, brushing crumbs off his clothes. 'It seems I was worrying over nothing. Come on, Sam, let's explore the cliff-top.'

'Be careful.' She wasn't sure for whom the warning was intended, Adrian or her son. Both of them, she decided. They made quite a picture as they walked hand in hand along the rim of the gorge.

She took her time packing the picnic things away, then followed more slowly to where Davina was staring dreamily out across the canyon. Slightly ashamed of harbouring such unfriendly feelings towards her, Jessie decided to make amends.

'It's a magnificent view, isn't it?' she asked, and Davina nodded. It was, indeed, a breathtaking sight. The gorge was about two metres across at the top and four metres wide at the bottom. The rocky walls plunged the height of a two-storey building to where the creek tumbled over rocks far below. To their right, a band of light played across a waterfall, the drops glistening like jewels.

Despite its innocent-sounding name, Meander Creek had been running high since the recent storms, and foam from the waterfall clung to the rocks.

'Where does the creek disappear to?' Davina asked, shading her eyes as she scanned the gorge.

'Do you see that rocky overhang?' Jessie pointed halfway down the gorge to a break in the vegetation. There, the creek crossed the canyon and disappeared under a vast shelf of living rock. 'It goes underground right there.'

'It looks like a white snake disappearing into its hole,' Davina observed. 'I gather it's not a good place to go swimming?'

Automatically, Jessie's gaze sought out Sam but he was safe, his hand tightly curled around Adrian's, as they peered over the edge of the waterfall. 'No, it isn't safe for swimming,' she agreed. 'Rock climbers love it because they can follow the creek underground, to some spectacular caverns.'

Davina shuddered. 'As one who suffers from claustrophobia, the idea has absolutely no appeal.'

Remembering Adrian's visits to these caves when the Grattons still owned the property, Jessie nodded. 'It's not my idea of relaxation.' She had been terrified every time Adrian disappeared into the earth's gaping black mouth, certain that she would never see him again. 'Let's walk,' she said, wanting to dispel the memory.

They strolled under a canopy of native trees, across ground cropped smooth by grazing kangaroos. None of the marsupials were in sight, but their tracks were everywhere.

'You're so lucky,' Davina said after a while.

Jessie's surprised look flew to her face. 'Me? How?'

On a heavy sigh, Davina said, 'You have it all—your career, your child, and Adrian.'

'You know that we're estranged, don't you?' Jessie was compelled to ask.

Davina's piercing blue eyes settled on her with the same forthrightness which had won her top ratings as a news reader. 'Not from where I sit. When he's around you, Adrian Cole doesn't seem all that estranged to me.'

Davina was mistaking familiarity for something else, Jessie was convinced. Still, she couldn't suppress the pleasure which surged through her at the idea. It also sounded unlikely that Davina was interested in Adrian for herself. Curiouser and curiouser...

'I love what you're doing with the house,' Davina said, surprising Jessie yet again.

The other woman's obvious sincerity was warming. 'Thank you. I'm having a great time restoring it to its former glory, but I can't take all the credit. The original designers deserve most of it.'

'Still, you're making it work in a modern context,' Davina said firmly. 'It isn't easy to combine the two, as I'm finding with my place. A lovely Victorian terraced house in the city,' she added.

'There's a lot you can do, provided most of the original features are intact,' Jessie suggested.

Davina grimaced. 'That's my problem. I'm surrounded by marble fireplaces, hand-painted tiles and etched glass. How do I combine them with twentieth-century comfort?'

They discussed the possibilities back and forth until Davina held up her hands. 'It's no use. I can't visualise it the way you can. You'll have to take my place on as your next commission, once you've finished Gratton Park.'

The idea of hiring herself out as a freelance interior designer was so novel that Jessie blinked hard. 'I hadn't thought of taking on more commissions after this one,' she said.

'Why not? You'd be working for yourself, choosing your own hours. And I have several friends I can recommend you to after my place.'

Could she do it? It was a gamble, but as she'd proved with Grattons, working for someone else offered only an illusion of security. And she'd be there for Sam when he needed her.

Excitement rippled through her. 'Maybe I could.'

Davina touched her shoulder. 'Smart girl. Let me know when you want to start.'

It was impossible not to like Davina, Jessie found. The idea of working for such a well-known woman was exciting in itself, but she also wanted to do her best for Davina as a friend. If it led to other commissions, that would be a bonus.

Fleetingly, she wondered if Adrian had had something like this in mind when he asked her to decorate Gratton Park.

Her reverie was shattered when Sam bounded up to her with all the enthusiasm of a St Bernard. 'Mum, guess where we've been?'

'No idea. Where?'

'Dr Cole and me climbed down to the entrance of the underground river. It's a 'normous cave with the water rushing right into it.'

Shock halted Jessie in her tracks. For the first time, she noticed the twigs and dirt clinging to his clothes where he'd been climbing through the bush. 'I don't want you going anywhere near that cave,' she said grimly, her fiery gaze coming to rest on Adrian, who had followed Sam back.

'It's all right, he was with me,' he assured her.

'And nothing could possibly go wrong while you're there, I suppose?' An edge of hysteria sharpened her voice. 'What if he'd slipped on the rocks, or fallen in, or...?' The horrifying possibilities finally robbed her of speech.

'I didn't fall. I was very careful,' Sam said, his childish joy evaporating in the face of her anger.

She dropped to her knees and hugged him. 'I know, sweetheart, but it's still dangerous. Promise me you'll never go down there again unless I'm with you.'

'But Mum...'

'No buts. Promise me.'

Sam's lower lip quivered, but he remained obstinately silent. Adrian stepped in. 'He doesn't want to promise because I said I'd take him into the caves one day.'

Jessie's startled gaze flew to his face. 'You what? You had no right to make such plans without consulting me!'

'And I intended to. The whole idea was conditional on your approval, wasn't it, Sam?'

The little boy gave a quick nod. 'Dr Cole did say we had to ask you first. But I can go, can't I, Mum?'

A leaden weight settled in the pit of Jessie's stomach. Was this madness genetic? She hadn't counted on Sam's inheriting his father's obsession with danger. She'd done everything she could to steer him in the opposite direction, emphasising academic pursuits almost to the exclusion of physical activities. Would blood out after all?

They were awaiting her answer. Slowly, she shook her head. 'I'm sorry, Sam. The answer is no.'

She heard Adrian's quick intake of breath. 'Just like that? No?'

'What do you expect me to say? He's only six years old, for heaven's sake.'

'So what are you going to do, wrap him in cotton wool until he's twenty?'

Sam tugged at her T-shirt. 'You have to say yes, Mum. You have to.'

Her eyes clouded as she turned back to him. 'I can't, darling. If anything happened to you, I'd never forgive myself.'

Sam's lower lip jutted out and a huge frown creased his forehead. 'You never let me do anything.'

'Yes, I do. I just don't want you doing anything dangerous.'

Adrian hovered over them like an avenging angel. 'It seems to me I've heard this line before.'

Was it so wrong to want to protect the people she loved? Was she supposed to sit back while her husband, and now her son, risked their lives in pursuit of some totally frivolous goal?

Well, she hadn't been able to stop Adrian doing it, but he wasn't taking chances with her son's life. 'Then you shouldn't be surprised to hear it now,' she said tartly.

With jerky movements which betrayed her annoyance, Jessie gathered the picnic things and shook out the rug. With his back to a tree and his knees gathered under his chin, Sam watched her, a mutinous expression on his face. He was angry with her for refusing to give in. One day he would thank her for protecting him, she told herself, as they made their way back to the house.

Adrian went on ahead, evidently as vexed with her as Sam was. Sam followed more slowly, scuffing the grass with his shoes, his head hanging. During the argument, Davina had discreetly taken herself off to admire the view. Now she caught up with Jessie to walk back.

Jessie was tempted to ask her whether she still thought the marriage had a chance, but decided against it. She was starting to like Davina, and didn't want to spoil the rapport between them.

Evidently Davina felt it, too. 'Thank you for letting me share your family outing.'

Jessie admired her ability to take the bad with the good. 'I'm sorry about the fireworks,' she said. 'But that's families for you. I enjoyed your company, too.'

Davina tossed her head back. The breeze caught her hair and unfurled it behind her like a banner. 'After a day like this, I wonder why I shut myself away in a sound-proof studio so much.'

'It wouldn't have anything to do with making a living?' Jessie speculated.

Davina laughed. 'Got it in one. But seeing you with Sam makes me miss my own family. My sister has twins about Sam's age.'

'Don't they live near by?'

'My sister's husband works on Thursday Island in Torres Strait, about as far from Adelaide as you can get,' Davina confided. 'It takes almost a week to get there, so I don't see them very often. And our parents seem to be on a permanent round-the-world cruise since they retired, so family gatherings are rare.'

'But you must lead a full life, being on television all the time.' Jessie recalled seeing Davina's face in the social pages countless times, at one glittering function after another.

Davina wrinkled her nose. 'The trouble with being on television is you can't tell who wants to be friends for your own sake, or because you have a famous face.'

'Any time you need a reality fix, you can come and join Sam and me. Better still, I'll lend him to you, an experience I guarantee will bring you down to earth.'

They were still laughing when they caught up with Adrian at the back door of Gratton Park. 'What's so funny?' he asked, wrestling with the big wrought-iron key in the ancient lock.

'Men,' said Jessie, and Davina rolled her eyes in agreement. When they started laughing again, Adrian shot Sam an impatient look. 'I can see this is at our expense. First one out of the bathroom gets the biggest ice-cream.'

Sam's sulky mood evaporated instantly as he raced Adrian inside to wash for the promised treat. Davina followed Jessie into the kitchen, and they began to unpack the picnic things. 'Adrian's good with children, isn't he?' Davina observed.

Jessie nodded. 'He always was.'

'Yet you didn't have any together?'

Averting her eyes, Jessie said softly, 'We couldn't agree on the timing. He was away a lot.'

There was a strained pause, then Davina said, 'I know it's none of my business, but I care about both of you. Do you think you'll ever get back together?'

Jessie's hands tightened around the handle of the wicker basket. 'Until recently, I'd have said no. But things have changed since Adrian came back from the jungle. The main thing we need is time.'

Davina's expressive eyes signalled her understanding. 'The space shuttle episode wraps up the current series of *Edge of Reality*. It will take the network a few weeks to decide if they want to commission a second series, so you should have some time together then. I'll keep my fingers crossed for you.'

The news that Adrian might soon have more free time came as a welcome surprise. 'I didn't know the series was almost finished. It's kept Adrian busy ever since he got back. For once, the time went quickly because he's been sitting in a studio, instead of going out on the expeditions himself. It's a pleasant change not to be worried sick about him.'

An odd light came into Davina's eyes. 'You don't know, do you?'

'Know what?'

The other woman seemed to realise that she was talking out of turn, and stood up. 'I'd better get going. I'm due at a fund-raising dinner at eight.'

Jessie clutched her arm. 'You can't leave without finishing what you started to say.'

'It isn't my place. If Adrian hasn't told you...'

'Told me what?' Her voice lifted. 'You'd better tell me. It doesn't look as if he's going to.'

Davina took a deep breath and exhaled slowly. 'I seem to be the bearer of bad tidings around you, Jessie. And I have a feeling this news definitely qualifies. Adrian was asked to do the final segment from the space shuttle as a civilian observer.'

Visions of the *Challenger* space shuttle exploding into flames rushed into Jessie's mind. 'Oh, dear heaven!'

'Of course, the project isn't set yet. There are a million details to be ironed out.'

But they would be, if she knew Adrian. Jessie felt sick to the depths of her being. Everything he'd told her about being happy to sit at home and let someone else conquer the mountains was a sham.

All too vividly, she recalled his resentment when the television crew had teased him about being put out to pasture. Here was his chance to get back into harness again and there was no way he would miss it if it was offered to him. Hadn't he spoken of travelling into space as the ultimate adventure?

Jessie hardly heard Davina let herself out. She was too busy reeling from this latest blow to her hopes and dreams. All this time, she'd worried needlessly about Davina, when there was another, more sinister rival on the horizon.

She had never been able to compete with Adrian's adventures before. How could she stand a chance against the siren song of the whole universe?

# CHAPTER EIGHT

'Sam won. He gets the biggest ice-cream.'

Her heart gave a giant lurch as Adrian wandered into the kitchen. His hair was slicked back where he'd run wet hands through it, and his skin glowed from his recent exertions. He looked relaxed and happy.

Was it the promise of going aboard the space shuttle which gave him an aura of well-being? It was as intoxicating as champagne, and if Davina hadn't told her the reason behind it, she could easily have imagined herself falling in love with him all over again.

Mechanically, she spooned ice-cream into glass parfait dishes and poured chocolate sauce on top. Sam, who'd followed Adrian into the kitchen, watched her, saucer-eyed.

'Did you enjoy your picnic?' she asked, pushing his ice-cream towards him.

He perched on a stool and dug into the treat. Adrian did the same, and Jessie noted wryly how alike they were in their enthusiasms. 'It was a good picnic,' Sam said solemnly, between spoonfuls. Then he frowned, 'But the river cave was the best.'

'I've already told you what I think about the cave. Eat your ice-cream, then you can read for a while before bed.'

'If you like, you can choose one of my books,' Adrian suggested.

Sam's eyes shone. 'One about rivers and caves?' His sidelong glance at Jessie dared her to object.

Adrian looked at her, and she nodded imperceptibly. 'I think there's a book on caving there somewhere,' he said.

They finished their ice-cream, then disappeared into the library, giving Jessie no chance to ask Adrian about the space shuttle. Would he get around to telling her himself? Or would it come as a *fait accompli*, like his other expeditions, with Adrian expressing surprise that she could possibly object?

The idea made her so angry that she slammed things around the kitchen as she restored order. 'Still mad at me for taking Sam down to the river?' Adrian asked, coming back into the room.

'You should have asked me,' she answered tautly.

'And I know what your answer would be.'

He was too much! She slapped a damp tea-towel against a counter-top. 'If you knew, it was irresponsible of you to go ahead.'

'What you mean is, I'm irresponsible,' he fired back. 'Or to be more accurate, anyone who doesn't toe your line is irresponsible. Correct?'

'You *would* think so, just because I object to you taking unnecessary risks with my child's life!'

He flung open the refrigerator door, took out a can of soft drink and opened it with a savage wrench. The popping noise sounded like a hiss of despair. 'He was perfectly safe with me. But there's the rub, isn't it? You don't want him to be safe with me. You prefer to keep him tied to your apron-strings, the way you tried to do with me.'

'I'm only doing it out of love,' Jessie said, not sure whether she was referring to Sam or to Adrian this time.

He tilted the can and drank straight from it, his profile so disturbingly masculine that she felt weak watching him. When he put the can down, droplets of lemon soda beaded his upper lip. She had an urge to wipe them away with her finger.

'You don't hold on to love. It holds on to you,' he asserted. His fingers tightened around the can. With one squeeze, he crushed it completely. 'This is what happens when you hold on too tightly. You crush the life out of it.'

She understood his meaning only too well. He'd accused her of crushing the life out of their marriage. Couldn't he see it from her side? She'd been alone when they married. Her greatest fear was of being alone again.

'Why are you two arguing?'

She hadn't heard Sam come in. Now he stood in the middle of the room, his eyes shadowed with distress. In his black, white and yellow Batman pyjamas, he looked small and vulnerable, his intellect no defence against the vagaries of adult relationships.

She gathered him against her. 'It's all right, sweetheart. Sometimes grown-ups disagree about things, the same way you and Nell disagree about things sometimes.'

Adrian ruffled the boy's hair. 'It's all over now, so why don't you go back to bed? I'll come and tuck you in myself. How's that?'

Sam brightened at once. 'First you have to kiss and make up, the way Mum makes Nell and me do,' he insisted.

'We could shake hands,' Jessie suggested.

The child shook his head. 'You have to do it properly.'

'I think we can manage it, don't you?' Adrian's gaze was dark as he loomed over her, lifting her to her feet with the slightest pressure of his hands on her wrists.

Mesmerised, she followed the progress of his mouth coming closer and closer, then he kissed her and the room began to spin. The universe spiralled in on itself until there was only the warmth of his hand against her back, the hard contours of his body aligned with hers, and the sweet taste of his lips devouring hers.

His hold barely slackened as he looked at Sam over her shoulder. 'Will that do?'

Behind her, she heard Sam's snort of disgust. 'I'm never fighting with Nell again if that's how you have to make up!'

It was all for Sam's sake, yet she couldn't help wondering if Adrian was as stirred by the kiss as she was. The moment he touched her, her senses went into overdrive. When he finally released her, she felt wrung out, as if she'd run a particularly gruelling marathon.

This would have to stop before it got any further out of hand. 'I'd better put Sam back to bed,' she said shakily.

'Do you like Dr Cole, Mum?' Sam asked, as she tucked him in.

She closed the climbing book he'd been studying, and set it down on the bedside table. 'Yes, I do,' she said, as honestly as she could.

'Are you going to marry him?'

Her legs gave way and she sank on to the side of the bed. It was time he knew at least part of the story. 'Dr Cole and I used to be married once, before you were born,' she began. 'But sometimes married people don't get along as well as they think they will.'

'But you get along now.'

'We're friends now. But you have to be much more than friends to stay married.'

'How much more?'

How did you quantify love? When did friendship become strong enough to bind two people in marriage? How long is a piece of string?

She dropped a kiss on Sam's sun-bronzed forehead and sighed. 'You ask some tough questions.'

Just when she thought he was drifting off to sleep, his eyes popped open. 'If you and Dr Cole got married again, would you let me go to the cave with him?'

Her heart gave a lurch of fear. 'I don't think so,' she said, more sternly than she intended.

He rolled over so his back was to her and she heard his muffled protest. 'It isn't fair.'

'Life isn't fair, darling.' How well she knew it. But he made no response, although she heard him brighten up when Adrian kept his promise and went in to say goodnight. Feeling left out, she showered and went to bed with a book, determined not to cross Adrian's path again that night.

He had already left for the studio by the time she got up next morning. Her night's sleep had left her more tired than before. Listlessly, she set about making breakfast and sandwiches for Sam to take to school.

He hated staying in bed, so she was surprised to have to go in and wake him. Usually he was up and about before she was.

'Sam, school time,' she called through his open door. When there was no answer, she went in. The covers were thrown back and the bed was empty. 'Sam?'

The bathroom was empty and tidy, a give-away in itself. Jessie felt the first stirrings of fear as she checked his clothes. They were gone.

A search of the garden revealed that he wasn't playing outside. Her fingers shook as she dialled the number of the television studio and asked for Adrian. When he answered, she explained that Sam was missing.

'Has he ever run away before?'

'Never. Oh, Adrian, what am I going to do?'

'You're going to stay calm. He can't be far away,' his authoritative tone rang down the line. 'I'll call the police from here—just as a precaution—then come straight home and help you look. But I'll bet he's at the gatehouse, fetching a favourite toy or some such thing.'

'You're probably right.' Tension threaded Jessie's voice. 'I'll check there as soon as I hang up.'

'By the time you've checked it out, I'll be with you.'

His promise buoyed her flagging spirits. 'Please hurry,' she urged, and rang off.

She made one more call to Jo, who had arranged to take Sam to school that day. She had a music class at Sam's school once a week and Nell looked forward to the days when they could travel together. Jo didn't hesitate. 'I'll be right over to help you look.'

'But what if Adrian...?'

'We'll worry about him later. Right now, you have to find Sam. I'll drop Nell off, then come straight over.'

'Thanks, Jo.' Jessie's voice was high and fear-driven. She slammed the phone down and rocketed out of the house. Sam had to be at the gatehouse. He had to be.

But he wasn't, and there was only one place left to look.

'The creek?' Adrian voiced her worst fear when he met her in the driveway, as she flew back to the main house. Sensing her panic, he grasped her wrists and forced her to look at him. 'Even if he went there, it doesn't mean anything's happened.'

'I shouldn't have forbidden him to go to the cave with you,' she wailed. 'If I hadn't been so stubborn...'

'He wouldn't have felt compelled to go by himself,' he finished, guessing her thoughts. 'You could be right but it doesn't help now. The most important thing is to get him back. I'll need some gear.'

She threshed helplessly in his grasp. 'There isn't time. We have to go down there now.'

Adrian hauled her towards the house as he spoke. 'We're more use to him if we're prepared. Trust me, Jessica. This is one time when you really don't have a choice.'

Of all the times he had asked her to trust him, this was the hardest. But he was right. She had no choice. If Sam needed help, they had to do it Adrian's way.

She allowed herself to be towed along in his wake, and watched helplessly as he threw ropes and other gear into a rucksack.

Finally, he picked up what looked like a child's snow sled. It was bright yellow and made of a lightweight foam, with ropes and handles at each side. 'Water sledge,' he said grimly. She couldn't bring herself to ask what use he expected to make of it.

With a screech of tyres, Jo pulled into the driveway as they were setting off. 'What can I do to help?' she asked, not waiting for introductions.

'Stay by the phone in case Sam turns up somewhere else,' Adrian instructed. 'You can also tell the rescue people where to find us.'

'Done and done.' Jo was white-faced but in control, and she squeezed Jessie's arm before she went inside.

The gorge seemed steeper and the creek more of a torrent than ever, when they reached it and peered over the rim. 'Sam, are you down there?' Adrian's voice rang hollowly across the gorge. There was no answer.

'I'm going down. Stay here,' he ordered.

Fear made Jessie reckless. 'I'm coming with you.'

A heartbeat passed while he registered her determination. 'Come on, then, but do exactly as I tell you.'

'Do we have to abseil down?' She'd never done it, and her knees shook at the prospect, but Sam might be down there. She would crawl over broken glass if she had to, to get to him.

'Thankfully, no. Sam and I found a route you can scramble down. Follow me.'

He made it as easy for her as he could, picking out hand and footholds, and guiding her limbs to them. Still, she was shaking by the time they reached the bottom—the scree, as Adrian called it. Tilting her head back, she surveyed the near-vertical drop. 'How on earth did Sam manage it?'

'We still don't know that he did. But determination is an amazing incentive, and he did have my book on climbing techniques. We both know what a quick study he is.'

Adrian was talking to keep her mind off what they might find, she realised, and blessed him for it. The sight of the creek, running high and foam-flecked, struck terror into her heart. What if Sam had fallen into it and been washed into the cave? Would they ever find him alive?

Tangled creepers curtained the entrance to the cave. Below them, the water disappeared into the earth's gaping maw. She looked at it and shuddered. 'Do you think Sam's in there?'

Adrian held up a tangled rope and a pathetically sodden blue object. 'I think so.'

'Hindsight!' She snatched the toy rabbit and cuddled it to her, tears mingling with spray from the creek. 'Sam must have brought him along for company.'

Adrian pulled steadily on the rope, which disappeared into the cave. 'He had the right idea, but it went wrong.' The rope snapped back against his chest, the ragged end painfully obvious. 'Cut through by a jagged piece of rock.'

'Oh, dear God.' Jessie crammed her fingers against her mouth to keep from screaming. In anguish, she began to tear at the creepers. 'We've got to get to him.'

From a wide leather belt, Adrian pulled out a long-bladed knife which gleamed wickedly in the morning light. Shouldering her aside, he slashed an opening in the vines, then looked back at her. 'Are you sure you want to come?'

With an animal snarl of protest, she plunged through the opening. Tangled in creepers at the top of a vertical step, she would have fallen headlong if Adrian hadn't grabbed her and steadied her. 'Better let me lead,' he said.

Shocked by her near miss, Jessie allowed him to go first, following the bright path of his torch into the underworld. In the darkness, the vegetation stopped and the rustle of wings began. Something brushed past her ear and she stifled a scream. 'Are you in here, Sam?' she called out.

Her voice bounced off the walls, but the only answer was the rush of the creek into its subterranean home. Adrian listened intently. 'There, did you hear it?'

'Hear what? Sam!' she called again.

This time she heard the faint response, like the rasp of chalk on a blackboard. 'It's him. It's Sam,' she half-sobbed. 'We're coming, darling. Mummy's coming.'

In the torchlight, Adrian began to lay out ropes and pulleys, and the yellow foam sledge. 'What are you doing? We have to go to him!'

His economical movements continued without pause. 'I am going to him. He's across the river, wedged in tree roots on a spit of rock.'

'Where? Show me,' she demanded.

'No time. If the river washes him off, we may never find him.'

'Dear God.'

It was agony to stand and watch, but it was all she could do as Adrian rigged up a pulley on the rope and attached it to the sled. Rigging a hook on the end of a rope, he ordered her to stand back. With great care, he cast the hook to the far shore with its rope in tow. 'This will be my guideline for the sledge,' he informed her.

Then he shrugged on a life-jacket and a helmet, from which a torch gleamed brightly. He handed her the other torch. 'If you know any good prayers, now might be an appropriate time.'

Jessie prayed as she had never prayed before, while he grasped the two handles of the sled, rested his chest on the foam surface and launched himself into the dark water. Like a cork, he bobbed across the water, gripping the guide rope to prevent himself from being carried away by the surging current. The light from her torch shook wildly as she tried to keep up with his progress.

A shriek tore from her throat as he reached for the tree on the opposite bank, and missed. He was carried several feet past Sam's position and her heart pounded agonisingly in her chest. Was she to lose both of them in this hell hole?

Suddenly he stopped moving. He had found a handhold on the opposite shore. Slowly and painfully, he hauled himself back against the current, to where she could just make out Sam's huddled form in the tree fork.

'I've got him.'

Her limbs gave way and she sank to the rocky floor of the cave. It was going to be all right. Adrian had asked her to trust him and she had, with her son's life. Those three words had justified all her faith in him.

But it wasn't over yet. Her anxiety mounted anew as she saw Adrian strap Sam to the foam sled. He was hurt! It was all she could do not to throw herself into the water after them.

It couldn't have been more than a few minutes before Adrian brought the sled with its precious cargo back across the river, clinging tightly to the guide-rope, but it seemed like an eternity before she was reaching for them, to help them from the water.

'Don't move him. Keep him absolutely flat,' Adrian commanded.

'What's the matter? Why isn't he moving?' This wasn't happening. It was a nightmare from which she was unable to wake up.

With infinite care, Adrian pushed the sled out of the water and placed it flat on the bedrock, then hauled himself out of the water and sat there, his arms draped over his bent knees.

The fight with the current both ways had exhausted him, Jessie saw. She touched his shoulder, feeling his powerful muscles quivering through his sodden clothes. 'Thank you for bringing him back to me.'

With a mighty effort, he heaved himself to his feet. 'Stay with him. The rescue team should be here by now, and they can move him safely.'

The horror of what he was suggesting flooded over her. He thought Sam's back was injured. The thought of Sam spending the rest of his life in a wheelchair was more than she could bear.

Sam stirred, testing the bond which held him to the sled. 'Mummy, my throat hurts.'

She caressed his damp forehead. 'Sssh, honey. We'll soon have you out of here.'

'Can you do something for me, Sam?' Adrian asked, with such gentleness that Jessie wanted to cry. Sam nodded, his eyes huge and glistening in the torchlight. 'I want you to see how still you can lie, without moving a muscle. OK?'

The child's trusting gaze met Adrian's. 'OK.' He became a statue on the sled, and Jessie marvelled at Adrian's influence over him. Where did it come from, this almost mystical bond between them? It had been there almost from the moment they met. Now it might save Sam's life.

The next few moments blurred as men in bright orange overalls swarmed into the cave. They brought powerful lights and a stretcher on to which they lifted Sam with the greatest care. She was gently but firmly moved aside, and watched apprehensively as they carried Sam out of the cave.

'I want to go with him,' she said, but Adrian restrained her.

'They have to winch him up the cliff as gently as they can,' he informed her. 'We'll only be in the way. It's better if we go up the way we came in, and meet the stretcher at the top.'

She was hardly aware of making the difficult climb back up, putting her feet and hands where Adrian instructed her to, and following his voice until they reached the top.

Cresting it, she was surprised to find that her legs refused to support her and she crumpled to the ground. Adrian dropped down beside her. 'It's only reaction. You'll be all right in a few minutes.'

The tears came then, spilling over with such ferocity that she was taken by surprise. She could only let them flow, gulping in air, until they stopped of their own accord.

'That's it, let it out.' Adrian massaged her trembling legs, the firm touch of his hands a welcome connection with the real world. Warmth flooded along her limbs, and feeling gradually returned to them.

'Think you can stand now?'

'If you help me.' She could do anything if he was there, she thought unexpectedly. His arm braced her as she got to her feet, as wobbly as a new-born calf.

He dropped a kiss on her forehead. 'That's my girl.'

The stretcher was almost at the top of the cliff. For the first time, she became aware of the throbbing beat of a helicopter, hovering nearby. It settled on the cliff-top in a tiny patch of level land, the rescue service markings vivid on its sides.

'They'll take Sam to hospital,' Adrian told her. 'It's the quickest and safest way to avoid further injury.'

'Can we go with him?' Jessie's anxious gaze fluttered to his face as she realised she was taking his presence for granted.

'Of course.' He looked down at his wet clothes. 'You go with the helicopter. I'll race home to change and drive across. I won't be far behind you.'

'Fine.' He asked the pilot where they would be taking Sam, then he waved and disappeared at a lope in the direction of the house. It wasn't until he'd gone that she remembered Jo was still there.

It was her first experience of travelling by helicopter. She would have been frightened to death if she weren't more worried about Sam, lying still and white-faced on the special stretcher strapped to the vehicle. The rescue people had stabilised him, but warned her that it wasn't wise to do much until the hospital gave its verdict.

The hospital had been alerted, and the staff sprang into action before the helicopter's rotors had stopped spinning. She was left to follow forlornly in their wake, as her son was whisked out of her sight.

She almost wept with relief when the waiting-room doors swung open and Adrian strode in. He hadn't wasted any time getting changed, but even in a pair of faded jeans and an ex-navy sweater, he looked heart-stoppingly attractive. Frantic as she was, she still noticed the nurses looking at him as he passed their station. She heard their murmurs of interest.

His arrow-straight progress never wavered. His hands descended on to her shoulders. 'Any news yet?'

Blindly, she shook her head. 'They took him away, and I don't know what's happening.'

Adrian's mouth tightened into a grim line. 'I'll see what I can find out.'

The nurses clustered around him, and Jessie saw them shake their heads, looking a little disappointed at not being able to help him. Then someone picked up a telephone and spoke into it. Twisting her handkerchief between nerveless fingers, Jessie wanted to rush over and demand to know what was going on. Instinct told her that she would learn more by letting Adrian handle it.

Moments later, a white-coated figure appeared, a stethoscope dangling from a side pocket. When he saw Adrian, his face creased in a smile of recognition and the two men shook hands. She stood up as they approached her.

Adrian spoke first. 'Jessica, this is Dr Asgard. He's handling Sam's case. Trevor was the medical officer on our last Antarctic expedition,' he explained.

She met the doctor's gentle gaze. 'Pleased to meet you, Dr Asgard. I'm glad my son's in good hands.'

'Trevor is the best,' Adrian assured her.

The doctor favoured him with a wry smile. 'Don't credit me with genius yet, Adrian. We still have to establish the extent of Sam's injuries.'

A cold sensation gripped Jessie. 'It's his back, isn't it?'

Adrian's hand came under her arm as she swayed. 'Not all back injuries are equally serious, are they, Trevor?'

'Fortunately, no. It's too early to tell, Mrs Cole, but in your son's case the prognosis already looks promising.'

'Then he won't be...' She couldn't bring herself to say the word.

'We don't know yet,' the doctor dashed her premature hopes. 'Why don't you two wait in my office until I have some news? Have a cup of coffee and try to relax.'

How could she relax when her son was injured, possibly even paralysed? Jessie wanted to resist, but lacked the strength, as Adrian led her down the corridor.

After the sterile unfriendliness of the waiting-room, the wood-panelled office was at least reassuring. She slid on to a leather-covered couch, and Adrian poured two cups of coffee from an ever-ready percolator.

'We're lucky to have Trevor,' he said as he handed a cup to her. 'He's a specialist in the treatment of back injuries. He's saved many sportsmen from paralysis by treating them with infusions of oxygen.'

'Is that what he's doing for Sam?'

'They're still doing tests to find out the extent of his injuries. It may not be as bad as you think.'

'I should have agreed to let him go to the cave with you,' she said tonelessly. 'It would have been safer.'

'At least you grant me that much,' Adrian said drily. Gradually, she became aware of the tension quivering through him. Why now, when the crisis was all but past?

'I should thank you for saving his life,' she admitted, putting her heart into the words.

Tension radiated from him as he stopped pacing, and looked at her. 'It was the least I could do, wasn't it, Jessica?'

She sniffed the air like an animal sensing danger. 'What do you mean?'

'You know what I mean. Today, I saved my son's life.'

She said nothing. He towered over her, his shadow plunging her into blackness. Suddenly he grabbed her wrists and hauled her upright, facing him. 'Sam *is* my son, isn't he?'

Was this nightmare never to end? She wasn't sure how much more she could endure. 'You can't prove anything,' she whispered.

His eyes blazed at her. 'Can't I? I've had my suspicions for a while, but today I met Joe—or Josephine, should I say? It was the final piece in the puzzle.'

'Even so, it doesn't prove you're Sam's father.'

'No, but Trevor Asgard will. I've asked him to run a DNA test on Sam.'

'A blood test isn't conclusive.'

'No, but DNA fingerprinting is. They break down a tiny fragment of tissue into its genetic components, something like a supermarket bar code. Every bar on a child's genetic fingerprint should match up with either the mother's or the father's DNA fingerprints. I expect it to prove conclusively that Sam is my son.'

Adrian's grip on her wrists was all that kept Jessie upright. She sagged in his hold, all the fight rushing out of her. Anger raced in to replace it. 'Your son, your proof . . . is it all that matters to you? Sam is my son, too.'

'You've had six years in that privileged position, Jessica,' he raged at her. 'Do you think I would have stayed away six years if I'd known he existed?'

So he would have come back for Sam, but not for her. 'I don't know,' she despaired. 'All I know is that I'm his mother, the only parent he's ever known.'

His gaze bored relentlessly into her. 'Then it's time we changed things, isn't it? I'm not a monster, despite what you think. I respect your role as Sam's mother.'

Hope rose in her. Was he going to be reasonable after all? 'Then you won't try to take him away from me?'

'Taking a six-year-old away from his mother is inhuman,' he asserted, but the tightening in his jaw warned her that there was more to come. 'He belongs with you . . . But he also belongs with me.'

'I can't give him up. I won't!' she denied fiercely, struggling in his grasp.

Adrian pulled her against him so hard that the breath was driven from her body. 'Then there's only one possible solution.'

# CHAPTER NINE

THIS was supposed to be the happiest day of her life, but Jessie felt utterly miserable as she prepared for the ceremony which Adrian had insisted on as part of his solution.

It was just as well she'd had her hands full visiting Sam at the hospital and helping with his physiotherapy, or she'd have run a mile rather than stand beside Adrian today in front of a marriage celebrant.

She would never forget her astonishment when she realised what his solution entailed. 'You can't mean us to start again where we left off?' she had gasped.

His gaze had never wavered. 'It's exactly what I mean to do. Sam has the right to a father as well as a mother. This is the only way to make it work.'

'But surely some sort of joint custody...'

'You mean you'd settle for that?'

Her hands fluttered helplessly in the air. 'Lots of couples do when there's no other way.'

'You'd be prepared to see Sam on occasional weekends?' he asked, with deceptive calmness.

An abyss deeper than the one in the cave had opened before her, black and horrifying, as she contemplated life without Sam. 'I didn't mean *I* would see him on weekends. I thought that you...'

'It isn't good enough for you, but it's supposed to be good enough for me, is that it?'

Jessie felt herself being backed into a corner. 'It's different for you,' she insisted. 'He's never known any other parent but me. You can't take him away from me now.'

His eyebrow lifted in a sardonic movement. 'Can't I? The courts are much more flexible about these matters nowadays. A father has rights, too. And his life with you hasn't always been idyllic, has it, Jessica?'

He already knew about the difficulties with Sam's schooling, and her frequent absences on business. If he wanted to, she had no doubt that Adrian could make her look like a poor mother in a court of law. What could she say in her own defence? I love my child, but I had a career to run? How would it look to an impartial judge?

'I'm not a monster, Jessica,' he went on when distress robbed her of her voice. 'I know you love Sam and he needs you. But he also needs me. Getting back together will give him a stable family background.'

What about her needs? He hadn't once mentioned wanting her to come back for herself. It was all for Sam, that was perfectly clear. She was a means to an end. It was a bitter pill to swallow. The real tragedy was, he had only to ask her to come back and she would have done so, with no need of coercion from him.

Witnessing his courage in rescuing Sam, she had finally admitted what she had kept from herself all along. Their marriage had never really ended, at least not for her. It had been interrupted by his absence, but the old feelings had returned in full force the moment she set eyes on him. She was deluding herself that it was over. In reality, it had barely begun.

Now he insisted that she become his wife again so they could share Sam's upbringing. Knowing how she felt, it was asking a lot. Yet the alternative was to walk out of his life.

Despite his threats, there was every chance she would retain custody of Sam, although the idea of fighting for her child terrified her. But the prospect of living without Adrian was equally disturbing.

The question was, could she settle for the little he was offering, knowing she wanted so much more? In a haze of uncertainty, she had heard herself say yes.

Adrian's response had been briskly practical. 'Good. We'll have the ceremony at Gratton Park as soon as possible so that Sam will have a proper family to come home to.'

Jessie's cry of protest was instinctive. 'I don't want any ceremony. It isn't as if we're divorced.'

'This is going to be public and official, for Sam's sake. Repeating our marriage vows will make them real and binding. You don't want Sam to suspect what's going on, do you?'

But neither had she counted on a public display which was entirely false. 'I don't know,' she said feebly.

'Take it or leave it, Jessica.'

A mutinous spark flared inside her. 'I'll go along this time, but you aren't going to blackmail me by threatening to take Sam away every time I refuse to toe the line. If it's to be like that, I'd rather get the court to resolve it now.' She hoped he wouldn't recognise her words as bravado.

He looked thoughtful. 'Fair enough, although I didn't intend to hold it over you. We were married long enough for you to know that I always play fair.'

She had to concede the accuracy of this. She might have fought tooth and nail against some of his plans, but he had never tried to conceal them from her, or lie about what he intended to do. 'I know,' she responded, in a hoarse whisper.

His hands were warm around her upper arms and the grip sent electric sensations arcing through her. 'It will be different this time,' he said earnestly, his gaze open and urgent as he looked at her.

How she wanted to believe him. But there was the news she'd heard from Davina Davis. With Sam missing and then injured, she'd had no time or thought to ask him about it. 'You can save your assurances,' she said tiredly. 'I know all about the space shuttle.'

His startled gaze raked her. 'Who told you?'

'It doesn't matter. The fact remains that it's true, isn't it?'

There was a strained silence, then he turned away. 'Yes, it's true.'

She wrapped her arms defensively around herself. 'What happened to making room on the mountain for someone else?'

'I was the one they invited. I'm surprised you even care any more.'

She did care, more than she was prepared to let him see. It was starting all over again, the old nightmare where she waited for a knock on the door and a message that he was dead. 'Now that Sam's found a father, it isn't fair for him to lose you again,' she explained. Maybe Sam could influence him where she couldn't.

His eyes bored into her, seeming to see every flaw in her argument. She wondered if he suspected the depths of her love for him. Desperately, she hoped not. If he knew, he would have no need of blackmail. She would be his, first, last, and always. But all he wanted was Sam. 'It's something to think about,' he said softly.

Jessie's hopes soared. Maybe Sam could influence Adrian where she had failed. Carefully, she kept the elation out of her voice. 'When shall we tell him about us?'

'As soon as the doctor says he's well enough.'

'He already knows we were married before,' she told him, and saw his look of surprised approval.

'He approves,' she said drily.

'Well, that's one of us,' he retorted.

Anger rose in her like a living thing. 'Don't expect me to be pleased, as well. Since I don't have any choice in the matter, I can hardly be over the moon about it.'

'Of course not. But I expect you to keep your feelings to yourself around Sam.'

He didn't need to remind her. She was the last person to put her son's recovery in jeopardy. What sort of mother did he think she was?

The doctor's office door opened to admit Trevor Asgard, Instinctively she moved closer to Adrian, feeling her face muscles tighten as tension radiated through her body.

Adrian's hand covered hers, his fingers tightening their hold. 'Well, Trevor?'

Beads of perspiration beaded the doctor's forehead, she noticed, as fear heightened her perceptions. He couldn't have been more than thirty, yet his skin was grey with fatigue, and there were violet smudges under each eye. When he smiled, the years fell away. 'He's going to be all right.'

Her knees buckled and Adrian's arm around her held her upright. 'Don't let her give way now, when the news is good,' the doctor said.

Clinging to Adrian was like clinging to reality. 'You did say he'd be all right. He will walk again?'

'Walk, run and jump. His back is injured and will take time to heal, but there's no nerve damage, so with time and the proper treatment he'll recover fully.'

'I don't know how to thank you, Doctor.'

Dr Asgard shrugged away her praise. 'Don't thank me. If Adrian hadn't been so careful getting him out of that cave, the outlook could have been much worse.'

Her eyes swam as she looked up at Adrian. 'You saved his life.'

Adrian's answering glance was solemn, but proud. 'He's my son; what else could I do?'

She would never forget the doctor's startled expression, but Adrian hadn't bothered to explain why he had no need to wait for the results of the DNA test to be sure. They had been allowed to see Sam for a few minutes before they were advised to go home so they could all rest, Sam included.

Now he was being allowed home for the ceremony, although he was still confined to a child-sized wheelchair, with instructions not to walk more than a few steps. A nurse had accompanied him home. Soon he would be home to stay, and Jessie had readily extracted his promise never to go near the creek by himself again.

'Dad's promised to teach me proper caving techniques,' he explained, with eyes shining.

How quickly Dr Cole had become Dad, she thought, with a pang. It was as if Sam sensed that it was real, although they hadn't yet told him the truth. As Adrian predicted, the idea of a wedding ceremony—actually solemnising their vows— thrilled him.

In his Sunday-best suit, seated in state in his wheelchair—which the nurse had decorated with ribbon for the occasion—he looked so small and vulnerable that she wanted to cry.

'Are you sure you feel all right?' she asked, noting his thin limbs and pale face.

'Yes, Mum. I want to come home, though.'

She dropped a kiss on to his forehead. 'Soon, sweetheart. When the doctor says you're all better.'

He brightened. 'They have a school at the hospital, did you know?'

'Yes, I know.' She'd made a point of asking Dr Asgard to occupy Sam's active brain during his stay in hospital.

'They have real big kids there. I can do some of their work,' he said proudly.

'Hey, slow down!' she said, forcing a laugh as alarm raced through her. What she really wanted to say was, 'Don't grow up too fast.' But she held her tongue. Gifted as he was, it was unfair to try to slow his progress, even if it meant robbing herself of his babyhood.

'How can I slow down when I'm not even moving?' he demanded, thankfully reverting to being six years old again, with a child's unassailable logic.

Jessie slammed the heel of her hand against her forehead. 'Silly me!'

Sam favoured her with a cheeky grin. 'I love you, Mum.'

Her gaze wandered to where Adrian was talking to the marriage celebrant. His dark suit and pearl-grey tie made him look more like a company director than a globe-trotting adventurer.

Her heart raced as she looked at him. After today, they would be husband and wife again. If only it was for real instead of for Sam's sake. She ruffled her son's hair. 'I love you, too, demon.'

At his urging, the nurse wheeled him in the direction of the buffet table. Watching them go, she was startled when a pair of hands descended over her eyes. 'Guess who!'

Jessie spun around. 'Susan! I'm so glad you could make it.'

Susan Gratton gestured to where her husband was talking to some of the other guests. 'Mark had plans to be in Cairns for the marlin season, but I told him your catch was more important.' She gave a theatrical wink. 'I think he meant to come all along, and wanted to make me suffer. He hates it when I'm right.'

Jessie suppressed a sigh. If it hadn't been for Susan's matchmaking, today's ceremony wouldn't have happened. She would have gone on raising Sam by herself and Adrian might never have known he existed. She wasn't sure whether to be glad or sorry it had worked out this way.

'You meant well, I know,' she said, kissing Susan's cheek affectionately.

Susan held her at arm's length. 'This is what you want, isn't it?'

Crazy as it seemed, it *was* what she wanted. She wished he felt the same way. 'Yes, I do love Adrian,' she replied with such sincerity that Susan looked convinced. 'Come on, I'll give you a guided tour of the house.'

Most of the decorating was finished. Only the bedrooms remained to be done, but they weren't needed for the reception.

When she saw the living-room, Susan gave a rapturous sigh. 'It's glorious—just what I dreamed of doing, but never got around to it.' She fingered a fall of curtain in a Sanderson cabbage rose print which dominated the room. 'You've made it modern and functional, while keeping the traditional feel.'

'Then you don't mind what we've done to the house?'

Susan's eyebrows arched. 'Good heavens, no, dear. It's a house, not a shrine. A woman must change things around to suit herself.'

On the way out, she squeezed Jessie's arm. 'I'm glad you and Adrian managed to work things out. This house needs a young family running around it. But you needn't thank me for selling Adrian the house. Being godmother to your next child will be thanks enough.'

Talking of children made it sound as if theirs was a genuine love-match, Jessie thought guiltily. As far as their friends knew, the fairy-tale ending *was* real. She and Adrian were the only ones who knew the truth.

She was saved from further complications by the arrival of Davina Davis on the arm of Tom Holland, the producer of Adrian's documentary series.

Introducing Davina to Lady Gratton, she left them in conversation and went in search of Jo and her new husband, Chris. Their daughter, Nell, was to be Jessie's attendant at the ceremony.

Jo looked uncomfortable when she approached. 'I feel as if this is all my fault,' she said, in a low voice.

'Adrian would have found out sooner or later that "Joe" was really Josephine,' Jessie assured her. 'You mustn't blame yourself. If anything, it was my fault for putting you in such a spot.'

'I didn't think. When you came back from the cave with Sam on a stretcher, I introduced myself without thinking.'

'And he put the rest of the story together himself,' Jessie concurred. 'The DNA test at the hospital only confirmed what he already knew in his heart, and what I'd said. Sam's his son and nothing can change it.'

She hadn't even told Jo that Adrian had insisted on a reconciliation so he could be a father to Sam. Her friend thought that now he knew the story about 'Joe' they had decided to give marriage another try, and she made no secret of her delight. She fairly glowed with the joy of her own union with Chris Napier and, being Jo, wanted everyone to be as happy as she was.

Chris took her arm now. 'We'd better sit down. They're getting ready to start.'

Left alone for a moment, Jessie scanned the group, unconsciously seeking one tall, broad-shouldered figure. When her eye lighted on him, a sense of rightness flowed through her. He might not mean the vows he was making, but she did. She wanted to be his wife again, and the mother of his son. Even though nothing had changed since they split up, *she* had changed. She wanted him on any terms, even those as unflattering as he had set.

Her head was high as she walked towards him. A curious light flickered in his eyes, then they were shuttered again, and she could read nothing in his solemn expression.

Her dress consisted of a lace camisole and lined skirt with a handkerchief hem-line, and a silk blouson top slashed to the waist and tied at one side. In pale ivory, it flattered her sun-kissed skin. With it she wore Adrian's wedding gift—a single strand of ivory-coloured pearls.

His look of appreciation warmed her as she took her place beside him. 'Ready?'

'Yes,' she murmured back, and gasped as his hand slid into hers. Against her heated skin his grip felt cool and reassuring, and her fingers twined in his.

He returned the pressure and she became aware of tension radiating through him, held deter-minedly in check. What was he tense about? Maybe he was afraid she wouldn't go through with this, and force him to fight for custody of Sam.

The ceremony was poetic and beautiful, and tears pricked the backs of Jessie's eyes as she responded.

The celebrant had modified the traditional wedding vows into a reaffirmation of their relationship. If only the words meant as much to Adrian as they did to her, Jessie thought. He responded unhesitatingly, in clear ringing tones, but she felt sure he didn't mean what he was saying.

'You may kiss your wife,' the celebrant concluded.

This time, Adrian did hesitate. Was he reluctant to prolong the charade in front of their friends?

About to turn away to hide her disappointment, she felt his palms gently cup the sides of her face. He bent his head and kissed each eyelid in turn, dispelling the moisture which clung to her lashes like dew. Then his lips found her mouth and the pressure intensified.

At his touch, tendrils of tormenting sweetness coiled through her. Instinctively she pressed closer. His hand cradled the back of her neck and she slid her own arms up to link behind him.

A sigh of satisfaction broke the spell. 'Now that's what I call a kiss.'

Her embarrassed smile found Chris Napier. 'Don't mind us, you two. Go right ahead,' he teased.

Jo nudged him sharply in the ribs. 'Stop it, can't you see she's blushing?'

The warmth on her cheeks came as a surprise. She hadn't blushed in years and the idea that her feelings for Adrian were so transparent mortified her. What if he guessed how she felt? Surely it wasn't part of his plans when he suggested they get back together? He'd made his feelings towards her quite clear when he'd confirmed his intention to go aboard the space shuttle.

He gave her an odd look as she moved determinedly away. Several times during the reception, she was aware of his eyes on her. Once, she caught the ghost of a smile playing around his lips, but it vanished when he saw her looking his way. He had reason to smile, she supposed. Everything had turned out just the way he wanted it.

A lavish buffet luncheon had been set up on a long table set up on the front lawn. They had been blessed with a glorious spring day, so there was no need for the marquee Adrian had hired on standby.

Jessie moved among the guests, ensuring they were well supplied with food and drink. When she reached Davina Davis and Tom Holland, they sprang apart like guilty schoolchildren. She could have sworn she'd seen them kissing behind the bushes a moment before.

'Looks like a day for romance,' she remarked.

Davina looked around, her expression alarmed. 'Did anyone else see us?'

Jessie schooled her features into a mask of innocence. 'See what?'

Davina gave a relieved laugh. 'Bless you, Jessica. We'd hate to read about our engagement in tomorrow's daily papers.'

'Even if it's true?'

Tom raised his champagne glass in a toast. 'Here's hoping it is. After months of my throwing myself at her, Davina finally deigned to notice me.'

She shoved him playfully away. 'You make me sound like a *prima donna*.'

'To me, you are, in the nicest possible way.'

Jessie stretched out a hand to each of them. 'I'm delighted for you both. I hope it works out for you.'

Davina nodded. 'It took us a while to realise we felt the same way. At least being in the same industry, we understand the pitfalls. But I'm not telling you anything. You and Adrian had to work these things out for yourselves, didn't you?'

If you counted avoiding the issues as working things out, Jessie thought grimly. And since she was the only one who wanted to work anything out, she didn't see much chance of improvement ahead. 'Every relationship is different,' she said, dismissing the subject. 'What do you plan on doing once you finish the *Edge of Reality* series?'

'We want to work together,' Tom said firmly. 'Actually, your Sam gave us the idea.'

Jessie's eyebrows arched upwards. 'Really?'

'Yes. He showed us how fascinated children are by the natural world, so we hope to interest the network in a children's science series.'

'We'd like Sam to be our technical consultant and tell us what kids are interested in,' Davina proposed.

Knowing how much Sam would love the idea, Jessie could hardly refuse, but her heart sank. It was another link in the mystical father-son chain which seemingly bound Adrian and Sam together. Would he want to climb mountains next?

'I'm sure he'd enjoy it,' she said weakly.

The rest of the day passed in a blur. Somehow, she said and did all the right things—even posing for photographs with Adrian's arm clasped around her waist as if it really were a happy occasion.

At last it was time for the guests to leave. Sam looked tired but happy, having spent the afternoon making paper planes and launching them from his wheelchair for Nell to chase. He didn't protest when Adrian suggested driving him and his nurse back to the hospital.

Desultorily, she helped the caterers, but only seemed to get in their way. Finally she decided to walk to the gatehouse to check on progress.

Adrian found her there, wandering from room to room, inspecting the new work. 'Happy with it?' he asked her.

'It looks lovely. I hadn't realised so many things needed fixing.'

'It's an old place. You'll want to keep it, of course.'

Did he mean them to go on living apart as before? 'I hadn't thought about it,' she admitted, with a quick flaring of alarm.

'You could rent it out to provide an income until your decorating business gets going,' he suggested. She had told him about Davina's proposal. 'I assume you'll want some financial independence from me.'

His thoughtfulness touched her deeply. In truth, she hadn't liked the idea of depending on him for everything.

'Thanks for thinking of it,' she said.

The corners of his mouth twitched as if suppressing a smile. 'I'm not entirely insensitive to your needs.'

For the first time in years, she felt shy and awkward in his company, as if they were indeed newly-weds on their wedding night. The words which usually came so easily stalled in her throat. She couldn't think of a single thing to say to him.

As if sensing her discomfort, Adrian took her hand. 'Let's go home.'

For a moment, confusion assailed her. This was her home, not Adrian's mansion. But she had taken solemn vows today and meant to honour them. Therefore, wherever he was was home. Without protest, she let him lead her back along the driveway.

The caterers had gone and the house drowsed, golden light from the lamps he'd left on spilling across the lawn.

Inside, he'd set out champagne in a silver bucket beside two engraved glasses. A dish of caviare nestled on a tray of toast triangles. In a side dish, the sight of enormous strawberries made her mouth water. 'What a feast!' she exclaimed.

'Your wedding feast, madam.' He guided her to a sofa and settled her on it, then ladled caviare on to a piece of toast and offered it to her. Nibbling it, she felt a thrill of intimacy which ignited into flames of desire as her lips reached the tips of his fingers. She kept nibbling.

In the lamplight, Adrian's eyes gleamed, and his breathing quickened. Reaching for a strawberry, he touched it to Jessie's lips, which closed around it. As she swallowed, she saw an echo of the movement in his pulsating Adam's apple. He drew a ragged breath and bent his head towards her, licking strawberry juice from her lips.

She tasted wine and caviare, and the salty tang of his maleness in his kiss. Hardly aware of what she was doing, she cupped her hand to the back of his neck and urged him closer. Expectantly, her lips parted, and she felt the seeking pressure of his tongue against her teeth.

'It's been so long,' she murmured, as need for him engulfed her. Buried desires resurfaced as raging demands which only he could satisfy.

'Much too long,' he agreed. His mouth seared a path across her throat and dived to the cleft between her breasts. She moaned softly.

The small sound was all the permission he needed. With swift movements, he shed his tie and shirt. His muscles seemed bronzed in the lamplight, and she ran eager fingers over them.

Explosive sensations ripped through her. She made no move to resist as he urged her upstairs to the waiting four-poster bed. His room was their room now.

They undressed in feverish haste, shedding clothes heedlessly to right and left; then he lowered her on to the bed, and she opened to him like a flower blossoming in the sun.

Whatever defences she had marshalled against him vaporised in the flames he ignited inside her. She was incandescent with longing for him. Every touch, every move fanned the flames until she felt molten in his embrace.

Telling herself it was just this once, Jessie allowed herself to feel rather than think, forcing herself to forget why she was his wife again. Fantasies of love flitted through her mind, driving her to a pinnacle of ecstasy which brought a cry of joy from her throat.

'Darling?' Adrian's loving concern tore at her heart.

She hadn't noticed she was crying until he brushed the tears from her cheeks with the back of his hand. 'I'm all right,' she said. Her tears were of happiness for what they had just shared, but she held back that part.

'As long as I didn't hurt you.'

Not physically, and that was what he meant. She shook her head and he pulled her into the warm curve of his body to wait for sleep.

It was a long time coming. She was still wide awake when she heard his breathing slow. Carefully, she shifted so she could drink in the sight of his strong features in repose, the dark lashes fanning his cheeks. Why couldn't it always be like this? Love was so rare, so precious. Surely he had room for her as well as Sam in his heart?

In the morning, she would tell him how she felt, she decided. The possibility of his rejection loomed large in her mind, but it was the only way. She loved him as he was, danger-man or no, and it was time he knew it. What if something terrible happened to the space shuttle and she never got a second chance?

# CHAPTER TEN

WHAT was so special about today? Jessie awoke feeling as if she had won the lottery. Every nerve in her body shrilled its happiness, urging her to throw back the covers and greet the morning.

Then it came back to her. Today was the first day of the rest of her life with Adrian. Last night they had sealed their new relationship with love-making so exquisite it was like poetry. It deserved the homage of complete honesty.

Today she intended to tell Adrian how much he meant to her. No mountain was high enough, no valley deep enough to stand between them. Those things were part of him, and she meant to love every part of him, not just the aspects she approved of. Maybe she could even teach him to love her, too, as he used to do.

Her shining eyes greeted her in the mirror, and she was astonished to see a golden glow which hadn't been there the night before. Her hand went to the slight curve of her stomach and excitement rippled through her. Last night might even result in a new child. They hadn't done anything to prevent it, and now she knew she didn't want to.

Showered and dressed in houndstooth trousers and a white silk shirt, she made her way to the kitchen. Adrian must have risen early, moving quietly to avoid waking her. His side of the bed was already cold when she woke up.

But he wasn't in the kitchen—although juice, a carefully segmented grapefruit and muesli were set out at her place. Propped up against the juice was a note, and she regarded it with a feeling of foreboding.

'Good morning, Jessica,' the note began. 'Sorry about this, but duty calls. No time to go into details but if you ring Tom Holland at the studio, he'll explain. Adrian.'

There it was. Not 'love, Adrian', just 'Adrian'. They hadn't planned a honeymoon, but somehow she'd thought... She certainly hadn't counted on him going to work as if this was any normal day.

Her happiness evaporated abruptly. Maybe it was, to him. He'd made his feelings clear: he wanted Sam and was prepared to remarry her to get his son. How could she have allowed the stars in her eyes to blind her to the facts?

With shaking hands, she dialled the number on Adrian's note and was put through to Tom Holland. He seemed tense. 'How are you this morning, love?'

'Confused,' she said levelly. 'Adrian has gone and he said you'd be able to explain.'

Tom swore softly down the phone, then apologised. 'I thought he'd told you yesterday. The space shuttle launch was moved up a few days and he had to fly out to Cape Canaveral this morning.'

Blindly, Jessie fumbled the phone back on to the cradle. Stupid, stupid, stupid! He'd made love to her last night knowing what he intended to do. An almost overwhelming sense of *déjà vu* assailed her. What if they *had* created a child, and something went wrong with the launch? She would be left to bear the child alone—just like the last time.

Good intentions were one thing, but reality another, she thought, as she rocked backwards and forwards on the kitchen stool. She wanted to support Adrian, but the old fears rolled over her in waves until she clenched her teeth to stop herself from screaming.

She was sitting statue-like in the kitchen when Jo breezed in. Taking one look at her set face, she swept Jessie into her arms and cradled her as she would her daughter, Nell.

Her concern broke down the last of Jessie's fragile reserves, and the latter wept bitterly, until there were no tears left.

'Feeling better now?' Jo asked briskly. She moved away and put the kettle on, then set out the tea things.

Jessie watched her impassively. 'No, just empty.'

'Like to tell me about it?'

Haltingly, Jessie explained what had happened. 'I want to wish him well, but ... all I can think of is ... what could go wrong. I keep imagining him injured or dead.' She buried her face in her hands.

'If you keep on like that, you'll never let him out of your sight,' Jo said sagely.

Jessie lifted a tear-stained face to her. 'Is that so wrong?'

Jo propped her elbows on the kitchen counter. 'Let me put it this way. What would happen to Sam if you never let him take the slightest risk?'

'He'd never learn or grow.'

'Exactly. We all need to grow as human beings, and no growth is without risk. Sometimes it's harder to be the one who watches and waits than the one who takes the risk.'

'You and Thorne?'

Jo nodded. 'When Thorne was in the police rescue service, I agonised over every imagined danger. He was highly trained, but still I worried. I decided to stop sitting at home, moping about it.'

Intrigued, Jessie leaned forwards. 'What did you do?'

'Went with him to prove to myself he could handle it.'

'You went on rescues with him?'

'You'd better believe it. I manned more roadside coffee-stands than you can imagine, just so I could be there. It wasn't pretty but I learned to trust him, and it beat the hell out of chewing my fingernails at home.'

'Were you there when...?'

'I've never told you this, but yes, I was there. Eight months pregnant and all. I held his hand until the last. And you know what? I'm glad. It was hell on wheels but it helped me come to terms with what happened. And I got the chance to say goodbye to him.'

By the time she finished, Jessie's eyes were as wet as Jo's, but this time she was crying for her friend, not for herself. She had also reached a decision. 'I'm going to the launch.'

Jo squeezed her hand. 'What took you so long?'

At the hospital, she found Sam in physiotherapy. Her heart swelled with pride as she watched him take a few wobbly steps between the parallel bars. His face lit up when he saw her. 'Did you see what I did?'

She pressed his face between her hands and kissed him. 'I saw, and I'm proud of you. You'll be home in no time.'

'It's not so bad. They have a pool here and it's hot.'

Swimming was part of his therapy, and Jessie nodded. 'Maybe we can get one installed at home. What do you think?'

'Our own pool? Wow! Wait'll I tell the other kids in the ward.'

She took a deep breath. 'Sweetheart, would you mind if I went for a couple of days?'

'Course not. I'm not a baby.'

You're my baby and always will be, she thought, but bit the words back. 'I know, and I'm proud of you. Auntie Drew will come and visit you while I'm gone, so you won't be lonely for long.'

He threw her a curious look. 'Are you going away with Dad?'

'He's already gone. I'm going to join him,' she explained.

'At Cape Canaveral?'

Suspicion gripped her. Was she the only one Adrian hadn't taken into his confidence? 'How do you know?' she asked.

''Cos Dad's going on the space shuttle and that's where it's launched from,' he told her. 'Dr Asgard said I can watch the launch on TV.'

'I'll wave to you from the crowd,' she promised, and gave him a farewell hug and kiss.

She was in tears by the time she left the hospital, but her resolve had never been stronger. This time she was going to be there for Adrian, whatever the outcome. If Jo could handle it, so could she.

The only flight she could arrange at short notice meant taking a domestic flight to Sydney very late that evening, then joining the big DC-10 which took her—via various stop-overs, and then with a change of planes—to Orlando in Florida.

Altogether, she was in the air for over twenty hours. She arrived at Orlando feeling drained and disoriented. Luckily, the time change between countries meant she wasn't too late to witness the actual launch.

As she wandered out of the baggage collection area, she was startled to hear herself being paged. But the only person who knew her destination besides Jo was Tom Holland, who'd given her the address of the hotel the studio personnel were using in Florida.

Apparently he'd contacted one of the station assistants who were working with Adrian's crew, and asked someone to meet her on arrival. 'This is very kind of you,' she said to the bright-faced young American who introduced herself.

'Tom said it was a surprise for Adrian, so we didn't mention you were coming,' the girl replied.

Relief surged through Jessie. She didn't want Adrian to know she was here until after the launch. Then she planned to travel to Edwards Air Force Base in California to be on hand when the shuttle touched down. Right now, he didn't need the distraction of her presence.

'Would you like to join some of the wives of the crew watching the launch?' the assistant asked Jessie.

Jessie's heart turned over. The thought of baring her soul to those wonderful, stoical women she'd

seen interviewed on television alarmed her. She
didn't want to be the one who turned to jelly the
moment anything went wrong. 'Look, I don't mean
to be unfriendly...' she began.

The girl smiled her understanding. 'This is the
first launch you've been through?'

'I'm afraid so.'

'I understand. You'd rather be by yourself. Don't
worry, I know how you feel. My dad's an astro-
physicist and I grew up around here, but I still remember the tension the first time he went up.'

She patted Jessie's shoulder. 'I have to get back
to work but the studio driver will drop you at the
hotel, or anywhere you want to go.'

Jessie nodded. 'Thanks for being so
understanding.'

She hadn't expected the luxury of a car and
driver. 'Would you take me somewhere?' she asked,
on impulse.

He touched a finger to his cap. 'Sure, ma'am.
Where to?'

'I'd like to see the shuttle. Is there somewhere
we can see it from?'

His face muscles twitched. 'You can see it anywhere within a five-mile radius of the launch site.'

'Oh. I had no idea.'

'I could take you to the grandstand on NASA
Causeway,' he suggested. 'You're cleared to be there
if you want to. They pipe a minute-by-minute
launch commentary through the PA system so you
can follow what's going on.'

She didn't want to be among the officials, for
the same reason she had refused to join the wives

of the crew. 'No, I just want to see the shuttle itself,' she emphasised.

Several miles from the launch site, the traffic became bumper-to-bumper. 'Why are all these cars here?' she asked.

'This is the most ambitious shuttle mission since flights resumed in September 1989,' he explained. '*Liberty* will fly to heights never before attempted, deploy a science satellite, and retrieve another. Everybody wants to be here. And there she is!'

They emerged from a depression in the land— where their view of the launch site was hidden by trees—to the sight of the dazzling white spacecraft, poised on the edge of the Atlantic. The majestic machine rose out of the Florida peninsula like an arrow aimed at the heavens.

In spite of her fears, Jessie felt her heart swell with pride at the thought of human beings soaring hundreds of miles above the earth in this great white bird. Emotions choked her, and she looked away.

'Gets to you, doesn't it?' the driver said, in an equally choked voice.

She nodded, too overcome to speak for a moment. When she regained control of her voice, she said, 'I'd like to go to the hotel now.'

When she checked in to her suite, she found a magnificent bouquet of flowers to greet her. A veritable cornucopia of fresh fruit spilled from a basket on the table.

Jessie buried her face in the fragrant blooms. What with Tom alerting the crew to her arrival, and the hotel's welcoming touch, she felt spoiled and grateful. She turned on the television set, and sat down to watch the launch.

A close-up view of the shuttle *Liberty* came on the screen first, almost as thrilling as her first sight of it in real life.

The camera panned across mission control, identifying various people involved with the launch. She waited in vain for a glimpse of Adrian, or any of the other 'payload specialists' as the announcer referred to them. One, a young woman who had apparently replaced an older astronaut who had failed the medical examinations, seemed to be the darling of the TV cameras. Jessie fumed with impatience as the cameras lingered on her.

Next came an announcement that the launch was to be delayed because of a problem with one of the shuttle's on-board computers. 'As long as this computer refuses to talk to the others on board, the launch is on hold,' the announcer came on-camera to explain.

'Never mind the computer, where's Adrian?' Jessie demanded futilely of the television screen. As if in answer, she caught a glimpse of him behind the announcer, crossing the floor of the mission control centre.

Then he was gone, and they announced that the launch would be delayed by several hours until the fault was found and rectified. The screen switched back to regular programming, and Jessie stared at it, wondering what to do now.

Every bone in her body felt weary, partly from the long flight to get here, and partly with the strain of waiting and wondering. Maybe Jo was wrong. Being here didn't make the wait any more palatable.

And yet ... there was something about knowing that Adrian was only a few miles away. If she wanted to, she could watch the launch from close range. It was her choice to seclude herself in the hotel, and knowing it was a choice made it easier somehow.

Aiming the remote-control at the television set, Jessie zapped it off. There was no point in watching endlessly when the launch might not take place for hours yet.

A call to the hotel switchboard ensured that she would be awakened when the launch was re-scheduled. It seemed they were quite accustomed to such requests, being a favourite hotel for people associated with the space centre.

'And by the way, thank the hotel management for the flowers and fruit. It's a delightful welcoming idea.'

There was a slight pause. 'Excuse me, ma'am?'

'The gifts left in my room. I want you to know how much I appreciate the hotel's thoughtfulness.'

'Of course, ma'am. I'll tell them.'

Strange, she thought as she replaced the receiver. The telephonist sounded as if she knew nothing about the flowers and the fruit. Maybe she was new, or they were a recent innovation. She gave a shrug and dismissed the whole question.

Blessed peace descended on her at last. She was here. There was no more she could do to show Adrian her faith in his decision. She decided to sleep until launch time, to try to regain some of her circadian rhythm.

Somehow, the dazzling light of the Florida day became the white snows on the slopes of Mount Everest. She had seen Adrian's photographs many times, after his expedition had conquered the southwest face of the mountain in record time.

Still, it was a surprise to find herself labouring across the Ice Fall in the wake of the other climbers. Her breath came in shallow gasps and every exposed part of her felt painfully cold.

Adrian called climbing the Ice Fall 'a cross between an assault on a medieval fortress and a stroll across a live minefield'. The chances of avalanche were ever-present.

They plodded ahead through towering gateways of ice, brushing aside slender icicles which tinkled past her to the valley floor.

Every few yards, ropes and ladders would be fixed in place so that if the area collapsed, their chances of survival would be greater.

Jessie wanted desperately to catch up with Adrian, who was in the lead. But no matter how hard she pressed herself in the thin air, the distance between them remained the same. 'Adrian, wait!' she called out. He looked back over his shoulder.

He stopped, and she thought he was waiting for her to catch up, but he was only helping one of the team to bridge a particularly wide crevasse. She quickened her steps. He was too far away. She should be with him.

Hurrying across the innocent-looking stretch of virgin snow, she suddenly dropped through a hidden hole. His horror-stricken look followed her as she threw her arms wide—the only thing which saved her from plunging all the way.

Adrian towered over her, hooking his powerful hands under her arms to haul her out. Looking down, she felt weak as she gazed into the hole. It was like looking into the nave of St Paul's Cathedral from the dome. The crevasse went down for hundreds of feet, vanishing into black shadows.

'Don't you know better than to walk about without being clipped to a rope?' Adrian railed at her.

'No, I don't. This is my first time,' she said, shaking with reaction at the narrowness of her escape.

He looked vexed. 'What are you doing here anyway? You should be at home with Sam.'

'But I want to be with you. Don't leave me behind.'

His anger abated and he regarded her with critical eyes. 'Is that what you're really afraid of? That I'll leave you behind when I go off on these expeditions?'

It *was* her deepest fear, she realised, allowing the thought full rein for the first time. She was afraid for him, but she was also afraid for herself, wanting to keep him with her, lest he succumb to the siren song of a mountain and never come back to her.

Her encounter with the crevasse had soaked her clothes. She shouldn't have tried to climb Everest in trousers and a silk shirt. She hugged her arms around herself. 'I'm so cold, Adrian—hold me, please...'

Oblivious to the stares of the Sherpa guides, who murmured 'Sherpani' at the sight of her, Adrian gathered Jessie into his arms. Warmth from him flowed into her, and slowly the shivering ceased.

She nestled against his chest, feeling the ice-encrusted fastenings of his jacket biting into her tender skin. 'You'll freeze out here,' he said softly into her ear. 'Let me take you home.'

'Yes please, Adrian,' she implored. 'Take me home. Take me home.'

'Sssh, I'll take you home,' he repeated, caressing her hair.

Gradually, reality seeped back and she stared blearily at him. Tentatively, she reached out a hand. 'I'm real. You were having some sort of nightmare, moaning about being cold,' Adrian said.

'I was cold. I was climbing Everest in a silk shirt,' she said ruefully.

He winced. 'Not your best idea, by far.'

She snuggled against him and sighed contentedly as his arms enfolded her. 'I only wanted to be with you.'

'You're with me now,' he said, in a strained voice.

The last of her jet lag left her and she struggled upright. 'You *are* here,' she repeated stupidly, absorbing the fact that she was in a hotel room in Florida. 'What about the shuttle launch?'

'Unless they get the computers talking to each other, the launch will have to be scrubbed. I decided not to wait around,' he said.

She searched his face, expecting to see regret there, but was astonished to find none. He looked the way she had visualised him climbing Everest— calm and relaxed, as if he was at peace with the world.

'You must be disappointed,' she said.

'Why should I be? I wasn't going anyway.'

She must be still asleep and dreaming. 'I don't understand. You said you were going.'

His mouth tilted up slightly at the corners. 'So I was. But not into space. Much as I would love to go aboard, I wasn't prepared to put in the necessary training. When I said I was coming here, it was to record the final episode of *Edge of Reality* from mission control.'

'Why didn't Tom or someone tell me?'

'They were under orders not to. I wanted you to think exactly what you did think, and come anyway.'

'Are you sure you won't regret turning them down?'

'Why should I, when everything I want is right here on earth?'

Another question burned in her brain. 'How did you know where to find me?'

He kissed the tip of her nose so gently that it was like a butterfly landing and taking off again. 'Who do you think sent you the fruit and flowers?'

'No wonder the hotel telephonist didn't know what I was talking about. I suppose Tom Holland tipped you off?'

'He didn't have to.'

Adrian wasn't making sense. 'Who else knew I was coming here?'

'Nobody. I just knew you'd be here.' A flash of uncertainty darted across his face, and was gone again. 'At least, I hoped you would come. Something in the way we made love told me you'd changed since I went away. I felt as if you were able to finally trust me enough to let me go.'

She touched the tip of his nose with a crooked finger. 'It wasn't a fair test. You left without asking me what I thought of the idea.'

'What would you have said?'

'I would have said "Go with God",' Jessie said in a choked voice, knowing it was the truth. 'I wouldn't have liked it, but I would have found the strength.' She paused, unsure whether to tell him the rest. 'Then I would have packed a bag and followed you. So it wouldn't have made any difference.'

'It makes all the difference to me,' he said. 'There were so many times I wanted you to back me up, but you were so set against my expeditions that you wouldn't have contemplated going along.'

'I finally realised your spirit of adventure is one of the things I love about you,' she admitted, in a cracked voice. 'Take it away and you aren't the same man.'

He clasped her arms urgently. 'Say that again.'

Her cheeks dimpled. She knew exactly what he wanted to hear but she couldn't resist teasing him a little. 'You mean about your spirit of adventure?'

He gave her a playful shake. 'You know damn well what I mean!'

Her eyes widened. 'Oh, you mean the part about loving you?'

'Damn it, woman, you are the most impossible...' He never finished the sentence, kissing her instead with a fierce hunger which sent tendrils of desire coiling through her.

'I do love you just as you are,' she said, when he allowed her to speak again.

'I know,' Adrian said, with a grin.

'How do you know so much?'

'You told me when we made love. There was no way you could hide your true feelings from me.

That's when I decided to lay a trail and see if you followed it.'

Pretending annoyance, she recoiled from him. 'You mean you lured me here? What did you have in mind?'

'I'll show you if you like, wife,' he offered.

He proceeded to do so with a skill which took her breath away. It was as if all the barriers between them had finally crumbled in the face of their love.

She had never known him to be so tender and passionate, sweeping her along on a tide of urgent longing until she was powerless to resist the waves of sensation which crashed over her.

They almost missed the shuttle launch when it finally happened. Cocooned in the warmth of his embrace, she had forgotten there was a world outside. Adrian kept his arm tightly around her as he reached for the remote-control and the majestic white spacecraft filled the screen.

'Shouldn't you be there?' she asked.

'Davina can manage this one solo,' he said, caressing the creamy fullness of her breasts. 'I have more pressing things to do.'

Jessie gave a deep sigh, and his anxious gaze flickered to her. 'What's the matter?'

'We've wasted so much time,' she said.

'It wasn't wasted if it helped us to find each other,' Adrian insisted. 'Sometimes adversity makes things stronger. In Africa, the monsoons can destroy whole tracts of land, but they also give life. The ground can be baked to cracking hardness, and as soon as the rain falls leaves and petals spring up almost as you watch.

'There's a particularly beautiful flower which grows everywhere after rain. It has spiky, brilliant red flowers so bright they almost hurt the eyes. They're almost four inches across and they spring up out of the naked soil after a downpour. The flower is called "wife of the rains".'

Jessie's gaze lifted to his face, exploring every dear and beautiful plane of it. 'Without the monsoon, there would be no flower. Is that what I am, a "wife of the rains"?'

His lips roved over her hair-line, and her stomach cramped in pleased response. 'You're all the more beautiful and precious now I have you back,' he agreed. 'I don't intend to let you go again.'

'Just try it,' she growled, and kissed the finger-tips dangling near her shoulder. 'Where you go, I go.'

'What about our child?'

'It could be children, plural,' Jessie teased. 'I didn't take any precautions when we made love.'

'Then they shall come, too,' he said decisively, 'although I can't think of anywhere I want to go now... I have too much to lose.'

The final moments of the count-down proceeded, and she watched the TV screen in fascination, then drew his hand down to her stomach. 'Do you realise, our son might grow up to be an astronaut?'

His hand moved sensuously over her skin, sending flares of desire shooting through her anew. 'Have you considered that it might be our daughter?'

As he bent to kiss her, his mouth giving and demanding all at once, she knew a moment of uncertainty. 'Are you sure you don't mind missing the launch?'

'How can I convince you that my adventuring days are over?' he demanded, and she arched her back in ecstasy as he made a valiant attempt. 'The hunter is finally home.'

*is*

 exotic

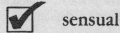 dramatic

 sensual

 exciting

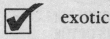 contemporary

 a fast, involving
read

 terrific!!

**Harlequin Presents—
passionate romances
around the world!**

# WELCOME TO

### The quintessential small town where everyone knows everybody else!

Finally, books that capture the pleasure of tuning in to your favorite TV show!

### GREAT READING... GREAT SAVINGS... AND A FABULOUS FREE GIFT!

Each book set in Tyler is a self-contained love story; together, the twelve novels stitch the fabric of the community. The covers honor the old American tradition of quilting; each cover depicts a patch of the large Tyler quilt.

With Tyler you can receive a fabulous gift ABSOLUTELY FREE by collecting proofs-of-purchase found in each Tyler book. And use our special Tyler coupons to save on your next TYLER book purchase.

Join your friends at Tyler for the sixth book, SUNSHINE by Pat Warren, available in August.

*When Janice Eber becomes a widow, does her husband's friend David provide more than just friendship?*

## HARLEQUIN
### Romance®

**Harlequin's Ruth Jean Dale brings you
THE TAGGARTS OF TEXAS!**

Those Taggart men—strong, sexy and hard to resist . . .

There's Jesse James Taggart in **FIREWORKS!**
Harlequin Romance #3205 (July 1992)

And Trey Smith—he's **THE RED-BLOODED YANKEE!**
Harlequin Temptation #413 (October 1992)

Then there's Daniel Boone Taggart in **SHOWDOWN!**
Harlequin Romance #3242 (January 1993)

And finally the Taggarts who started it all—in **LEGEND!**
Harlequin Historical #168 (April 1993)

**Read all the Taggart romances!
Meet all the Taggart men!**

Available wherever Harlequin books are sold.     DALE-R